Mrs. J. H. Riddell

A struggle for fame

A Novel. Vol. 2

Mrs. J. H. Riddell

A struggle for fame
A Novel. Vol. 2

ISBN/EAN: 9783337046378

Printed in Europe, USA, Canada, Australia, Japan

Cover: Foto ©Andreas Hilbeck / pixelio.de

More available books at **www.hansebooks.com**

A

STRUGGLE FOR FAME.

A Novel.

BY

MRS. J. H. RIDDELL,

AUTHOR OF

'THE MYSTERY IN PALACE GARDENS,' 'GEORGE GEITH OF
FEN COURT,' ETC.

IN THREE VOLUMES.

VOL. II.

LONDON:

RICHARD BENTLEY AND SON,

Publishers in Ordinary to Her Majesty the Queen.

1883.

CONTENTS OF VOL. II.

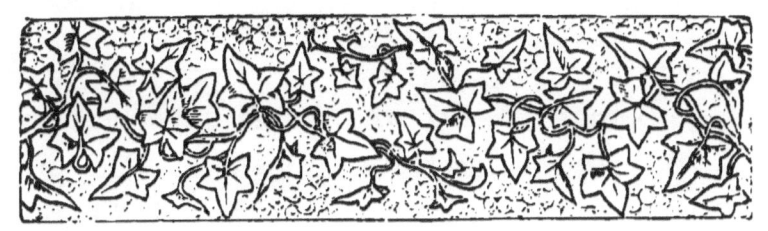

A STRUGGLE FOR FAME.

CHAPTER I.

MR. KELLY'S DAY.

AS best he could Mr. Kelly whiled away the hours till one o'clock, when, according to agreement, he met Mr. Dawton, and was by him introduced to the editor of the *Galaxy*, a periodical which not long before had been started under good auspices. Amongst its contributors were numbered the best men of the period. On every page sparkled wit, talent, high spirits, high thought—now dead, or grown old and very feeble. It was a most excellent magazine; stories, poetry, articles, were all admirable.

Bernard Kelly, who would have been glad to procure insertion anywhere, felt proud beyond description to think he should appear before the public in such capital company. 'How's Maria?' had indeed done something for him.

'What about the Government office now, eh?' the head of the Dawton family had said one day when he encountered his new friend in the street; and Mr. Kelly answered only with a smile which told he accounted the loss of his uncle's patronage a gain.

As it was the fortunate author's intention to return to West Ham to remove his effects from beneath Mr. Donagh's roof that same afternoon, he declined all young Dawton's blandishments and invitations; but while they stood together in Fleet Street arguing out the question whether or not Mr. Kelly should regard The Wigwam in the light of a short cut back to Stratford, they were joined by three other congenial spirits, all of whom likewise were what they called 'members of the same gang.'

Just at the same time, Mat, after a most satisfactory interview with the manager of the

Galaxy, which had resulted in the transfer of a goodly amount of current coin of the realm into his pockets, emerged from the office, an .air of holy calm pervading his countenance, a saintly smile flickering about his lips, and his whole deportment that of a man at peace with himself and the world at large.

As he passed the group Will Dawton and one of his friends spoke and nodded to him, while Mr. Donagh returned their salutations with befitting dignity. Had the matter ended there, all would have been well; but one of the others, turning his head to see who was thus greeted, recognised a familiar presence, and called after the retreating figure:

'Well, old fellow! and how goes it?'

At the words Mat looked back, and saw not merely the man who uttered them, but Barney Kelly—Barney evidently hand and glove with these gay 'swells'—Barney, with a laugh frozen in his throat at sight of the man he had parted with on such bad terms some fifteen hours previously.

Here was in visible presence the haunting terror which had made Mat's life of late a weariness to him. Here he met that 'ruffian' in the last place he desired to see him, and amongst the very set of people he most dreaded his knowing. He had presence enough of mind for most accidents, but it failed him now. There were few things he could not face, but he felt it impossible to make the best of this encounter. With a smothered reply and an almost involuntary wave of his hand, he turned on his heel, and diving down one of the narrow streets leading southward, was immediately lost to view.

'I did not think you knew him!' exclaimed Mr. Kelly.

'Know him!' repeated Will Dawton, to whom the remark was addressed. 'Of course we do. Everybody knows him.'

'But you told me you did not.'

'Nonsense! you are dreaming, man. When did I ever say anything so ridiculous?'

'The night I asked you about him you said you knew no one of the name.'

' 'What name?'

'His name—Donagh.'

' But that's Mat—majestic Mat, marvellous Mat, miraculous Mat, mendacious Mat.'

'Of course, Mat Donagh.'

Young Dawton took the speaker by the shoulders, and looked him straight in the face.

' Is that your friend ?' he asked.

' Yes. That is he—what does he write ? Oh ! for heaven's sake, Dawton, satisfy my curiosity.'

' I really don't know,' answered Will Dawton, with a pleasing reticence.

' I don't think he writes anything,' interposed one of the others ; ' he touts for advertisements.'

' What is that ?' asked Mr. Kelly.

There was a roar of laughter at this question, and then young Dawton said :

' Pray treat Mr. Donagh's name with due respect, Myers. He is a most important factor in the success of the *Galaxy*. Truth is ' —he went on, speaking to Bernard Kelly— ' your friend is the best advertisement canvasser in London.'

' What is an advertisement canvasser ?' inquired Mr. Kelly, whose ignorance on most subjects connected with literary matters was almost as great as his curiosity.

Will Dawton answered the question. In a few telling sentences he explained, adding, that though possibly the *Galaxy* might exist without its 'crack' novelist or sledge-hammer leader-writer, or sportive essayist, or tender poet, or cynical reviewer, it could not live without Mat. Understanding the cause of the gloom which overshadowed Mr. Kelly's countenance, he good-naturedly went even further, and implied that while it might be practicable, though difficult, for the *Galaxy* to secure such another editor as it happily possessed; though a double to the present efficient publisher probably existed in London, yet a second Mat could never be found, so bland, so winning, so persuasive, such a favourite, even with the roughest of advertisers; such a treasure, in fact; such a very mine of wealth, indeed, to the journal which had been fortunate enough to secure his services.

All these utterances Mr. Kelly received with a show of satisfaction he was far from feeling. The assurance that Mat could net his five hundred a year 'without turning a hair,' capped by a further hint from one of the company that he might easily double the amount named if 'he chose to stick to it,' scarcely filled his heart with that pleasure the statement ought to have aroused.

'Mat came to London, I have heard, meaning to make a great splash in literature,' proceeded the last speaker; 'tried prose and poetry both, hacked about for a while on the *Somers Town Sentinel,* and did slating notices for the *Peckham Pioneer,* but he could not get on as he expected, and therefore adopted what he calls his present profession. He says it was quite by accident he took to it; but, however that may be, he makes a deuced good thing out of the work. And he is so high and mighty into the bargain. He won't do this, and he can't accept that, and his peculiarities have to be humoured, or off he goes. We poor devils of authors are forced to study the fads and whims of publishers and editors. In our case the boot is quite on the other leg. What do you say, Dawton ?'

Will Dawton laughed.

'I don't think you study anybody's whims,'
he answered ; then, turning to Bernard Kelly,
added, 'I suppose your friend has a snug crib
down at—what is the name of the place—
West Ham ?'

'He lives in a good house,' replied Mr.
Kelly.   He was not going to disparage Mat's
habitation to these lively young men, or
correct them as to the amount of that gentleman's income, which indeed, for all he knew to
the contrary, might have been princely.

'And where did you get to know him,
Kelly ?'

'He comes from my part of the country.
His ancestors were great folks once upon a
time.   There is a place not far from Callinacoan that goes still by the name of "Donagh's
Leap ;" no man and horse, before or since,
could take it.   They were a rare wild lot, the
Donaghs of Castle Donagh—went through their
money and their acres at the same rattling pace
they followed the hounds.'

'Anyone could tell at a glance Mat had
come of a good stock,' observed one youth
who wore a glass screwed into his right eye.
'There is a sort of "keep your distance" about

his manner which I confess always impresses me.
Well, I suppose some must go up and some
come down. It's only fair, old families should
have their noses brought to the grindstone, in
order to let the newest snob have his turn.
Every dog has his day, and I dare say Mat's
forbears had theirs.'

'Yes; he was saying just the same thing
no later than last night,' answered Mr.
Kelly, privately reflecting that his day was
come. He could meet Mat now on his native
heath. He knew, if nobody else did, that his
host was groaning in spirit, weeping and
wailing and gnashing his teeth at the idea of
that 'uncultivated boor Barney' having at
length come to the comprehension of what he
did—the kind of literature to which he devoted
most of his shining hours.

In good truth, Mr. Donagh was more annoyed than words could express; not even
the money in his pocket reconciled him to the
notion of Barney knowing how he got it.
There did not exist a human being he less
desired to become intimately acquainted with
his affairs than the guest he had persisted in
inviting to Abbey Cottage, whom he had not

treated civilly, and who was now in a position
to smite him hip and thigh with a weapon
snatched from Mat's own especial armoury.

'What a cursed casualty!' he considered, as
he wended his way to a tavern he wot of in
the heart of the City, where the steak was of
the juiciest, the ale mellow, the cheese ripe,
and the port unexceptionable.

In such modest haunts he managed to get
rid of a good deal of superfluous cash, but
on the occasion in question no appetite appeared with the viands.   Barney Kelly had
destroyed his relish for food — Barney, who
with one slight kick could destroy the lordly
castle Mr. Donagh was supposed, by those
who knew no better, to inhabit—Barney, who
at last understood exactly ' what he wrote,' the
true nature of the manuscripts which, figura-
tively thrust under the domestic pot, kept that
utensil boiling.

Contrary to his usual habit, it was scarcely
five o'clock when he put his latch-key in the
lock and let himself into Abbey Cottage.
Miss Cavan had ' just closed her eyes between
the lights, and was taking a bit of a nap.'
Miss Hester did not chance to be in, having

'stepped across to the Broadway for a pen'orth of tape;' but the maid-of-all-work, hearing the master's step, looked out into the hall, and, in answer to a question concerning Mr. Kelly, said :

'No, sir, he has not gone yet—he is up in his own room.'

Mat, full of the purpose which had brought him home so early, straightway ascended the stairs and knocked at the door of his unwelcome guest's bedchamber.

'Come in!' cried Mr. Kelly lustily, with a dreadful cheerfulness in his tone.

Mr. Donagh went in, and found the objectionable Barney in his shirt-sleeves, kneeling before a portmanteau he had filled to overflowing and was struggling to lock. A solitary dip illumined the apartment. Amongst the many things which had not been done at Abbey Cottage was laying the gas upstairs; and in the exercise of that economy which was evinced by saving at the spigot and spilling at the bung, the Donaghs had got into the habit of considering one candle enough in all conscience for any man, and more than enough for any single woman.

As Mat entered, Mr. Kelly looked up.

'You are back early,' he remarked.

'Yes,' agreed Mr. Donagh, as he closed the door.

He paused for a few moments before he spoke again—moments Mr. Kelly utilized in forcing the portmanteau to fasten. He was busy with the straps when his host said :

'I conclude you now know the secret of my life.'

'I am sure I cannot tell,' answered Barney carelessly ; 'I know how you earn your bread, if that is what you mean.'

'Yes, that is what I mean—you have learnt how, in order to supply the most vulgar and ordinary wants of existence, a Donagh has been compelled to forget the traditions of his family, and descend so far in the social scale as to accept a commission for the orders he is able to wring from reluctant and paltry trades-people—men the very fact of whose existence his ancestors would scarcely have deigned to recognise.'

'There is not much use in talking about your ancestors,' replied Mr. Kelly, rising and planting one foot on the portmanteau, so as to get a better purchase of the strap he was wrestling with. 'I think you ought to consider yourself a deucedly lucky fellow, Donagh, though your only " connection with the Press" is through the medium of the advertisement columns.'

Mat waved his hand with a deprecating gesture, and shook his head mournfully, the while he said :

'The heart knoweth its own bitterness, and with the gall and wormwood of mine no stranger may intermeddle. I had my aspirations, I had my day of proud hope, my conviction of eventual success in the highest walks of literature, but between promise and fulfilment intervened the cursed necessity money—money to provide food and raiment—to satisfy grasping landlords and impracticable collectors of rates and taxes. But why prolong this agonized explanation ? I beheld all my soul had longed for—all my higher nature had panted to reach and possess—engulphed in the vortex of carking household cares—of common domestic wants in which ere now many a nobler ship than mine has foundered.'

'Well, it can't be helped,' observed Mr. Kelly indifferently, looking round the room to see which of his belongings he had best begin cording next. 'What's the good of crying over spilt milk? And you have been very fortunate, Donagh; it is not everyone who fails in literature that has the luck to find such easy and profitable work as you have taken to.'

'Easy!' repeated Mat scornfully. 'Profitable! yes, truly, I do make a sufficient yearly income; but I did not come to you intending to complain of my lot, or to ask sympathy for blighted hopes which once blossomed fair and gay—no! my object now is to entreat your forbearance — your chivalry. Those poor women below still believe in me. They know nothing of the horrible depths to which I have descended. Let them remain happy in their childlike ignorance—let them in their innocence cull the flowers which have sprung from the grave where my genius lies buried, and sport with the blooms which have their roots in my broken heart.'

Mr. Bernard Kelly, accustomed as he was to Mat's figures of speech, stood transfixed during the delivery of this final sentence, which was uttered in a subdued voice, and with a touching humility. When Mr. Donagh paused a spell seemed broken, however, and he answered:

'It is too late ; I have told your aunt what you do.'

'Miscreant!' exclaimed Mat passionately ; 'ingrate, to rush home and sting the bosom that warmed you!'

' There was no particular reason why I should keep your counsel,' said Mr. Kelly carelessly. 'You had it in your power to help me, and you took very good care not to do so. You might have got me on the *Galaxy* long ago, and now I am writing for it ; no thanks to you.'

'Writing for the *Galaxy!*' echoed Mr. Donagh. Amidst all his trouble he had never dreamt of this additional misfortune.

'Yes, my friend, "'tis e'en so,"' answered Mr. Kelly. 'I assure you I haven't found my accent or nationality the slightest hindrance to me in literature ; quite the contrary.'

Having received which fresh arrow in his broken heart, Mat turned slowly, and without uttering another word left the room.

It was three hours later. Mr. Kelly had
taken his departure—or, as Miss Cavan tersely
observed, 'the house was shut of him'—and the
ladies were seated at needlework when the
master of Abbey Cottage, who had declined
to partake of tea with his relations, or to allow
a cup to be sent in to him, suddenly abandon-
ing the seclusion of his sanctum, appeared in
the parlour.

Walking up to the chimney-piece, he took a
commanding position, with his back resting
against the marble slab. Neither Miss Cavan
nor Miss Donagh spoke. They saw that in his
face which held their kindly tongues silent.

'Girls,' began Mat, and his features twitched
a little as he uttered this inappropriate word.
'You know the worst now. Do you despise
me?'

'Despise you?' repeated both in a breath;
and next instant two fond, foolish, faithful
women were clinging round his neck, sobbing
out endearing phrases, and conducting themselves altogether in a most idiotic manner.

'Ah! you poor souls!' exclaimed Mat, wiping
his eyes—for he was really deeply touched—
'Why did I leave it to Barney Kelly or Barney

anybody to tell you the story of my lost life
and marred career? Why didn't I trust you
from the first?'

'Ay, why didn't ye?' asked Miss Cavan,
and then they all fell to weeping again. But
after a time the luxury of sorrow began to
assert itself, and they settled down to the enjoyment of their misery in the most comfortable manner possible.

The ladies felt that it was their own Mat
they had got back at last, while Mat, 'now
that the felon irons of silence and dissimula-
tion were struck off his spirit,' revelled in telling
the story of how he had 'conquered fate.'
With bated breath and eyes fastened eagerly
on his face, Miss Cavan and her niece hung
enraptured on his accents, and listened en-
tranced as he spoke of the 'lions' he had found
lurking in his path, of the difficulties he, a
second David, had taken by the throat and
killed.

'And indeed it's yourself could make your
way, if it was even through stone walls,' exclaimed Miss Hetty admiringly, while her aunt
opined Mat's energy was so tremendous that a
'dungeon could not contain, or fetters bind it.'

Never, perhaps, had the household at Abbey
Cottage spent so pleasant an evening. Mat
off his stilts seemed quite a different person
from Mat up in the air. He was quite 'affable
and familiar.'

'Though Barney let out what he did for
nothing but spite,' said Miss Cavan, with that
quick perception of motives which, as Mr.
Donagh was good enough to declare, 'distin-
guishes the feminine mind,' 'he did us a good
turn. If he knew how comfortable and cosy
we all are he'd be ready to bite off the end of
his tongue for envy. Ye'll never keep anything from us again, Mat, no matter how bad
it is, will ye?'

Mat declared he would not, which was a
very large and a very unwise promise; but at
the moment he had no mental reservations—
his heart was full of gratitude and com-
punction.

'How could I ever have been ashamed,' so
ran his thoughts, 'of these admirable creatures,
who combine in their own persons every virtue
of their sex? Why did I sacrifice to society
that which should have been offered on the
altar of home?'

Possibly it was with some idea of even at the eleventh hour repairing this error that Mr. Donagh presently suggested they should have a 'morsel of supper together in peace and comfort.'

Suppers did not much obtain in that house, and were rarely of an impromptu character, being, as a rule, confined to Sundays, Easter, and Christmas.

Mat partook of so very few meals at home that the ladies seized upon his idea and adopted it with the delight of children bidden to a feast.

'Thanks to Mrs. Kelly, there's plenty and to spare!' exclaimed Miss Cavan; and proceeding to the kitchen, which was vacant, the servant having retired to bed, she soon 'tossed up a little repast' her nephew assured her was a *chef-d'œuvre.*

Very merry were they all, and very happy, and in such unwonted spirits that when Mr. Donagh, who was told by Miss Cavan, 'You must have a glass of punch to-night, Mat, though Barney is not here to take one with you,' said he should not touch a drop unless she and Hetty partook of some also, the poor

lady, who scarcely ever drank anything stronger
than tea which had stood brewing till it was
bitter, answered he might, if he pleased, mix
her and Hetty a very very little, only he must
be sure to make it 'as weak as weak.'

Which was accordingly done, after an appro-
priate remark from Mat concerning the time-
honoured joke 'Hot, strong, and sweet,' and
then, to the end that aunt and niece might not
seem to be 'sitting down to punch regularly,'
they drank the seductive beverage out of
one tumbler, which gave rise to a running fire
of—

'I've had as much as I need, Hetty.'

'Nonsense, aunt.'

'Well, I'll just put my lips to it.'

'Go on.'

'If I take any more I shan't find my way to
my bed.'

'Mat, you've put twice too much whisky
in.'

'Have a teaspoonful.'

'Not a drop.'

'Wet your lips.'

'I'll have half if you will,' and so forth, till
it was all gone, and Miss Cavan had washed

and polished the tumbler and 'put it past' carefully, so that Mary's weak morals might not be destroyed by such an awful example on the part of her mistresses.

Poor simple women—dear, honest, kindly souls—what a trial you must have proved to any man save the one for whom you would cheerfully have laid down your lives ; and yet how exactly you suited him and adapted your-selves to the many angles and twists of his complex character !

CHAPTER II.

LADY HILDA'S HUSBAND.

EANTIME Mr. Vassett's path could hardly have been considered one strewn with roses.

He had got into the thick of a difficulty, and did not exactly see his way out of it.

'The next time,' he said to Mr. Pierson, 'the next time I have anything to do with a lady, and that lady a lady of title, you may write me down anything you please.'

'One swallow does not make a summer,' returned the reader, who, having given it as his deliberate opinion that 'some day' the 'Irish girl' would 'make her mark,' did not mean to eat his words or retract his advice, 'to encourage her.'

But Mr. Vassett was adamant. ' Have we
not had enough of petticoats?' he asked. 'Men
can't deal with women in business matters. If
her ladyship were of the other sex ¡I'd know
what to say to her, but as it is——' and a
gloomy silence enfolded the conclusion of Mr.
Vassett's sentence in mystery.

' She is a slippery customer, as I always
thought,' observed Mr. Pierson, speaking as if
he had prophesied the exact trouble which had
occurred.

' You never thought she would serve us the
scurvy trick she has done.'

' Why don't you go and see Hicks?' asked
the reader. Mr. Vassett shrugged his shoulders
with a gesture of distaste.

' What's the good of writing about such a
matter? You could tell him more in five
minutes by word of mouth than it would be possible to explain by letter in five months.'

' I do not feel disposed to seek an interview
with Mr. Hicks. As a business man, there can
be no question he will consider I have acted
with culpable carelessness.'

' Pooh !' exclaimed Mr. Pierson. ' As the
happy husband of his wife, he must under-

stand the nature of the lady who has let us into this hole better than we could be supposed to do.'

'I am inclined to imagine his intimate acquaintance with her peculiarities will not make him look more favourably upon my part in the transaction.'

'Shall I go and beard the citizen in his den?' asked Mr. Pierson. 'He can't put me in the Tower, or take me before the Lord Mayor, and I don't care what he says. Hard words, you know, break no bones.'

Mr. Vassett remained silent for a minute, casting this suggestion about in his mind; then he said:

'No, I shall first write. A letter will serve to open the ground, at any rate.'

'And when shall you open the ground?' inquired Mr. Pierson, with the suspicion of a sneer.

'This day,' answered Mr. Vassett, speaking determinedly.

'And what do you intend to say? Shall you tell him the high jinks her ladyship has been playing?'

Mr. Vassett winced visibly under this dreadful expression.

'I wish, Pierson, I really do wish——' he was beginning, when the other cut him short.

'Yes, I know you do; but never mind that now. Are you going to say exactly what has happened, or is it your intention to lead him gently on till you consider he is prepared to hear he will have to fork out——'

'Pierson! Pierson!'

'Nearly double the amount he was led to expect,' finished Mr. Pierson, resolute not to amend his expression, but to complete the sentence in its integrity.

'All I mean to indicate in the first instance,' replied Mr. Vassett, with as much dignity and precision as a severe cold in his head would allow, 'is that I find it will be necessary to lay before him a difficulty which has arisen in connection with the novel placed by Lady Hilda in my hands for publication. We shall then hear what he says in answer, and my future course will be to a great extent guided by the terms of his communication.'

'I can't see the use of all this diplomacy,' remarked Mr. Pierson, in that disparaging tone which never failed to rouse his chief's temper. 'Why not go to the man at once,

and explain the trick his wife has played you ?
Bless you, he won't be astonished ! He must
know her. He is perfectly well aware there is
no sort of cheating she is not up to. Better
take a 'bus into the City to-morrow, and get
the matter off your mind at once. That's
what I should do.'

' Is it ?' said Mr. Vassett. ' Then it is what
I should *not* do.'

' Oh, of course you know best.'

' Yes, I imagine I do. Rapid and violent
measures are always, in my opinion, to be
deprecated.'

Mr. Pierson looked at the speaker and
smiled, as he said suggestively;

' If much time is expended on this interesting correspondence you will have Lady
Hilda coming here to know why she has not
received the remainder of the proofs.'

' Should her ladyship come, I shall know
what to say to her,' observed Mr. Vassett.

' All right ; only don't ask me to help you
out of that scrape.'

' I am not aware I am in the habit of either
getting into scrapes or of asking you to help
me out of them.'

Once again Mr. Pierson smiled. There are times when a smile is more irritating than a blow, and Mr. Vassett felt at that moment as if he could not endure his reader's impertinence much longer.

'You allow yourself too much license of speech, Pierson,' he said coldly.

'Do not confound me with Lady Hilda, pray,' entreated Mr. Pierson. 'When she swoops down here for proofs, you will know more about license of speech than you do now. However, it is not my business, thank goodness! What have we got here?' he added, thinking it prudent to change the subject, and turning over some newly arrived manuscripts Mr. Vassett had brought downstairs and laid on his table. '"Three Years in the Southern States of North America," by Sir Richard Draper, M.P. What is that about?'

'You had better see,' answered Mr. Vassett, with less urbanity than usual.

'"From Mexico to Moscow," by an ex-Diplomatist,' proceeded Mr. Pierson; 'who on earth wants to know anything about either Mexico or Moscow?'

'A considerable number of persons, I should say,' observed Mr. Vassett loftily.

Mr. Pierson glanced up for a moment with a very good semblance of surprise, and then continued :

'"Sitella : a Life - Study," by Gregory Bacon. Why, I returned that a week ago.'

'So the author writes. He says he knows you did not read it, and that he returns the MS. to enable you to do so.'

'Set a trap, I suppose ?' remarked Mr. Pierson, with unmoved composure ; 'turned a leaf upside down, or left a scrap of silk between two pages. I did look at the opening and the wind-up ; it is rubbish. "Reminiscences of the Footlights," by S. Dawton. You will look them over yourself, I suppose. "Six French Actresses," by C. Cheshire— Cheshire Cheese.'

'I think that may be worth attention,' remarked Mr. Vassett, ignoring the attempt at wit involved in this transposition.

'It is clean, clear copy, at any rate'—commented Mr. Pierson, reconciling himself to the inevitable. 'And here is another "specimen,"

I declare, from our young Irish friend—" The Next Heir "—not a bad title.'

'Send it back at once,' interposed Mr. Vassett, with a firmness worthy of St. Senanus, 'as well as the other manuscripts of hers you were speaking of. We'll have no more women here.'

'Lady Hilda! Lady Hilda! What have you not to answer for!' said Mr. Pierson, shaking his provoking head with solemn waggishness, as he gathered up the bundles of manuscript, and retired with them to his sanctum—a little room built out at the back of the premises and lighted from the roof, and which had possibly been a tool-house in the days when gardens, but no publishers, were to be found in the select seclusion of Craven Street.

Rid of his reader, Mr. Vassett began to indite his letter to Mr. Hicks. Though he said little more than he had indicated when speaking to Mr. Pierson, the epistle occupied some time in the composition, for not merely was the theme one on which it seemed to the publisher inexpedient to commit himself, but in addressing a citizen — a man who was 'merely wealthy,' or as Lady Hilda expressed herself, 'disgustingly rich'—Mr. Vassett's pen assumed almost unconsciously an elegance of diction, a choice of phraseology, and an ambiguity of style intended to produce an impression on Mr. Hicks, who went as straight to the point as a bull at a red rag, and who had about as much talent or taste for diplomacy as, once again to quote from his wife's forcible vocabulary, 'a mad dog.'

The situation was indeed painful to the publisher 'in his capacity both as a man of sense and a man of business.'

Very early in their acquaintance with Lady Hilda he had so far gauged the character of that fascinating individual as to induce him, in order 'that subsequent complications and misunderstandings might be avoided,' to obtain from Mr. Hicks an authority to expend a certain agreed sum which might fairly be presumed to cover all expenses connected with and attendant on the publication of a three-volume novel.

Her ladyship's idea of the nature of the partnership of matrimony may be gathered from the fact that she stipulated all profits

arising from the sale of her books were to be
paid over to her without deduction of any
kind—not the net profits, be it understood,
but the gross—and even when this was done
faithfully, not merely for love of honesty, but
for fear of the authoress, she grumbled and
scolded, and accused Mr. Vassett in very plain
and vigorous English of cheating her. She
tried hard to make him pay for the press
copies, while as for allowing the publisher to
keep a copy for his own reading, and in pleasant memory of their agreeable relations, as
he courteously suggested, Lady Hilda would
not hear of it. She said she could never
understand why she was defrauded out of the
retail price. The novel was advertised at
thirty-one and sixpence, therefore why did
she not receive a guinea and a half? Pitched
battles had she and Mr. Vassett over this
question, and also the 'thirteen as twelve'
which figured in his accounts.

'It is all nonsense,' said Mr. Vassett, 'talking to me about a woman not comprehending
business. What she cannot see is justice, so
long as half-a-crown is to be made by remain-
ing blind.'

Nevertheless, as has been said before, he was proud of having Lady Hilda's name in his list, and if he did not get meal out of the wife he got malt out of the husband ; therefore, though he and her ladyship were always quarrelling, they had rubbed on together 'fairly well,' as the Scotch say, till she took it into her head to write a book he could not publish without the certainty of being dragged into several actions for libel.

Even one action for libel being a possibility too terrible to contemplate, he set his foot down, and compelled Lady Hilda for once to yield her point and allow the obnoxious paragraphs to be expunged.

Duly and truly Mr. Pierson, who in common with his principal entertained, not without reason, the gravest doubts of her ladyship's good faith, toiled again through the manuscript, erasing all personal and questionable suggestions, and reducing the novel to a level of dull propriety which might have satisfied the requirements of a bench of bishops.

At this point, considering he had seen enough of the book to satisfy his curiosity for the present, he relinquished all respon-

sibility. Where the works of authors he
deemed important were concerned, it was Mr.
Vassett's practice to run through the proofs
himself, only referring to Mr. Pierson when
he thought some change might be effected
with advantage.

The reader, however, prepared manuscript
for the press with such care and judgment
that, as a rule, no corrections had to be made
in Craven Street. The author saw to all those
which were necessary, and it need scarcely be
added that whatever other mistakes the printer
might fall into, he was never guilty of the
omission of not charging for even the slightest
alteration in the text.

For a time, then, Lady Hilda's latest
novel had proceeded joyously through the
press.

No matter how long a publisher may have
elected to keep a book back, there always
comes a period when he wishes to get it out
without delay. This is the case at the present
moment, and this was the case in the very different era when Lady Hilda had the field of fiction,
comparatively speaking, to herself. Mr. Vassett having heard of an important work being

' in preparation ' by a rival house, desired to get the start with Lady Hilda's novel. Then, as now, the librarians had only a certain amount of money to spend ; and then, as now, they did not like spending that certain amount if they could avoid doing so.

Quite aware of this, it seemed good in Mr. Vassett's eyes to hurry on the printers ; and, accordingly, proofs came fast and thick to Craven Street, and were posted every day to Lady Hilda.

The proofs were not returned for press from Craven Street, but they were from Lady Hilda's residence ; and as fast as she returned the sheets her corrections were attended to, and the book printed off.

The first volume was completed, the second also, and the third was half-way through, when, at the printing-office, the attention of one of the principals was drawn to the enormous number of author's corrections in the novel—corrections which not merely involved the alteration of sentences and the necessity for revises, but the re-imposing of pages, and in some cases the almost entire resetting of chapters.

Taking up one of the proofs, black and almost illegible by reason of her ladyship's emendations, in order to satisfy himself there was reason in the complaints made on this subject, he saw enough to induce him even at the eleventh hour to inform Mr. Vassett of the increase in expense he might confidently look forward to.

' Lady Hilda has almost rewritten the novel,' he said.

Mr. Pierson did not happen to be in the way when this communication reached Craven Street, but within five minutes of its receipt Mr. Vassett was *en route* to Soho—and for a quarter of an hour after he arrived at the printing-office it might have been thought the end of the world had come. Everyone was talking at once—explaining, recriminating, remonstrating; men in paper caps were running hither and thither, clasping soiled revises in their blackened hands. All the compositors seemed wanted in a hurry; the manager displayed corrected proofs; boys scurried about after perfect copies—there was such a to-do it might have been thought the Father of Mischief himself had got loose among

24—2

the type and was setting up broad-sheets by
the score.

'There is one comfort, Mr. Vassett,' said
the head partner at length, meaning to be
consolatory, 'we discovered the matter in time
to prevent publication.'

Mr. Vassett could bear no more. He was
known as a publisher of mild and courteous
manners, not given to strong language or many
words ; but on the occasion in question, though
he did not say much, what he did say was to
the purpose, and there was an energy in his
diction and a concentration in the one sentence with which he flung himself out of the
office never to be forgotten by those privileged
to hear.

All those goodly reams of double crown
wasted, all that composing, and re-imposing,
and re-setting, and revising, and re-reading,
and printing off, worse than useless ! all the
advertisements thrown away ! Mr. Vassett
felt as if he should go mad.

And then arose the extremely interesting
question : 'Who was going to pay for this ?'

The printers had given him clearly to understand they did not mean to lose their money ;

from Mr. Hicks Mr. Vassett only held a guarantee for a certain fixed amount ; from Lady Hilda it was vain to expect anything except gibes and insolence ; and there was one thing quite positive, Mr. Vassett did not intend to pay the bill himself.

Under the circumstances, therefore, it will be seen some necessity for diplomacy existed.

' You are fond of exercising a little strategy,' Mr. Pierson was ill-natured enough to say. ' Here is a capital opportunity :' and then ensued the conversation recorded at the beginning of this chapter.

Poor Mr. Vassett ! Well might he declare the next time he had anything to do with a woman's book the sky would fall. No wonder he told Mr. Pierson peremptorily to return Miss Westley's manuscripts.

' I call it a piece of great impertinence on her part,' he remarked later in the same day, ' to continue sending me a chapter or two as a " specimen." As I have told her, no one can form an opinion unless a whole book is submitted for perusal. Authors nowadays seem to think publishers exist simply for their convenience.'

' As far as the rejection of manuscripts is concerned,' said Mr. Pierson, ignoring Mr. Vassett's general statement, and confining himself to the special iniquity of which Miss Westley had been guilty, ' I can form an opinion as well from reading one side of copy as a whole book. The acceptance is quite a different matter.'

' Pierson, you are talking nonsense,' said Mr. Vassett, not, perhaps, without reason.

' At any rate,' replied Mr. Pierson, ' I shall not tell the girl she must send in a three-volume novel before I express an opinion on her work.'

' Tell her to send nothing,' answered Mr. Vassett. ' If I cannot get manuscripts I care to publish from men, I will cease to publish.'

But Mr. Pierson did not obey this command. He returned Miss Westley's ' specimen ' with a little kindly word of encouragement.

' She'll do something yet,' he considered ; ' but she may wait a little—waiting does not hurt them.'

By ' them ' he meant authors, and more especially lady authors. He had never tried authorship himself, and he knew nothing of the long-drawn-out sickness of hope deferred, which though it may harden the tree—takes the bloom off the fruit, and renders success when it comes quite a different thing to what youth believed it would prove.

When we grow tall enough to gather the grapes that once hung high above our reach, the taste is not what we imagined we should delight in ; but, after all, is not this the case with all the grapes of life—wealth, love, fame, happiness ? If we could only realize at the beginning what poor things in reality the clustering bunches we spend our strength striving to grasp, are in fact, what a vast amount of trouble we should save ourselves long before we arrived at the end! Only in that case we might probably do nothing ; and so it is best for men and women to go on hoping and believing, even though the close of their day should find the sun setting amid clouds of disappointment.

Even a publisher has disappointments. Remember that, O discouraged authors! and take heart again. If the children of this world, in the shape of hard and stern capitalists, have their losses and crosses, how can writers, over-apt to consider themselves children of light, expect to find the literary road easy under foot, bordered with shady trees, and fragrant with sweet-scented flowers?

The next day Mr. Vassett received Mr. Hicks' answer to his diplomatic mission. The happy husband's reply ran as follows :

' DEAR SIR,

' I must ask you to explain the nature of the difficulty you mention to my solicitor, Mr. Daunt, Crosby Square, who, I trust, will be able to arrange matters with you satisfactorily.

' Yours faithfully,

' T. HICKS.'

' This is dreadful,' thought Mr. Vassett. To explain the matter to Mr. Hicks had seemed bad enough, but to explain it to a vague solicitor, one of a class he regarded with laudable misgivings, seemed impossible.

' Now you see you ought to have taken my advice, and gone in person to the fountain-head,' observed Mr. Pierson, when he was told what Mr. Hicks said.

' I had better write and explain the state of the case,' suggested Mr. Vassett feebly.

' You had better do no such thing,' retorted Mr. Pierson; 'see this Daunt man at once, and get the thing off your mind. For my own part, I think you ought to feel thankful a solicitor has been imported into the question, for he may perhaps stand between you and Lady Hilda.'

' I can't go anywhere with this dreadful cold,' said Mr. Vassett, coughing as much as he could, and striking his chest pathetically.

It was deferring the evil day, and Mr. Pierson knew this, but he only answered:

' There is no time to be lost. Shall I go ?'

' No; it will be better for me to write,' coquetted Mr. Vassett.

' For heaven's sake don't commence a correspondence which may continue for a year,' entreated Mr. Pierson. ' Let me go and try the ground. I promise you I won't say a word that can implicate you.'

It was some time before Mr. Vassett would listen to this suggestion; and if he had not dreaded receiving a visit from Lady Hilda before he knew in what way to deal with her,

the reader would probably never have carried
his point.   Mr. Pierson was extremely fond of
meddling in matters which one would have
thought in no way concerned him, and on a
few occasions he had consequently proved really
of use to his chief.

'After all,' considered Mr. Vassett, ' he can
speak about what I have done for Lady Hilda,
and all I have suffered at her hands, as I could
not possibly speak myself. His brusqueness will
probably not offend a lawyer as it might a husband ; and, on the whole, it is perhaps prudent
to put the affair in train as soon as possible.'

For these reasons, and for another much
more cogent than any of them, viz., that he
did not want to go himself, Mr. Vassett at
length graciously yielded an apparently reluctant consent to the course proposed.

Fearful of any change of mind if he allowed
time for the publisher's mental thermometer
to vary, Mr. Vassett, though the rain was
coming down in torrents, set off at once, pooh-
poohing all suggestions as to the advisability of
delay, and saying for his part he would rather
catch a cold than that Lady Hilda should catch
them unprepared.

'For she will insist on the book being published, you may depend on that,' said the reader, buttoning up his overcoat preparatory to leaving Mr. Vassett to consider at his leisure the extreme likelihood of these words proving prophetic.

Several hours elapsed before Mr. Pierson returned—he had waited to see Mr. Daunt, he had also lingered to dine, and loitered to partake of something hot to keep out the cold.

He was dripping with wet—he looked spare and hungry as ever—and his appearance would have done credit to a man who had been fasting for a long time, and did not exactly know where his next meal was to come from ; but there was a buoyancy in his step and a twinkle in his eyes, and a self-satisfied expression on his face which assured Mr. Vassett he had to some extent, at all events, succeeded in his mission.

'Well ?' said the publisher.

'Well !' answered Mr. Pierson, provokingly reticent.

'Did you see Mr. Daunt ?'

'Yes, and had a long talk with him. By Jove ! it was lucky I went.'

'Will they pay the money?' asked Mr. Vassett, anxious to hear Mr. Pierson's "luck" had assumed some tangible and desirable shape.

'Oh yes, that will be all right,' said Mr. Pierson carelessly. 'Daunt is going to advise Hicks to make no fuss about it—but what do you think? *Hicks wants her ladyship to go back to him!'* .

'You don't mean that?'

Yes, I do; and I have undertaken to get her to go back.'

'You will never induce her to do anything of the kind.'

'Shan't I? We shall see.'

CHAPTER III.

MR. PIERSON 'RECEIVES.'

T was a most miserable day in the miserable February of 1855. The snow which had fallen previously lay still on the horse-roads. A way had been cleared through it on the side-paths, but only in a perfunctory manner, and pedestrians were compelled in many thoroughfares to walk single file between frozen banks of mud. The sky looked black and heavy, as if laden with more snow. Sleet and rain drifted in the faces of the passers-by; while a damp cutting wind, swirling round corners, and rushing down cross-streets, and raking the main arteries of the metropolis, bade defiance to topcoats, and at times rendered umbrellas worse than useless.

A most miserable day, indeed, to be abroad ;
but then what day during the early part of
that year proved otherwise ? and it was with
a pleasurable glow of satisfaction that Mr.
Pierson, ensconced in Mr. Vassett's own office,
looked at the fire he had just stirred up to a
blaze, which went flaring up the chimney, and
glanced around the comfortable room where
for the time being he was monarch of all he
surveyed.

Mr. Vassett was upstairs with a cold, the
newspaper, and his correspondence ; and during his compulsory absence from business Mr.
Pierson occupied his office, sat in his especial
chair, piled coals on his grate, stood on his
hearth, and warmed himself, and, looking out
at the wretched weather, reflected gladly he
was not as those poor sinners who were forced
to trudge the streets and get soaked with mire
and rain, but snugly housed in a room which
was well furnished, and cosy, and free from
draughts, and which, moreover, he was paid
for sitting in, and doing very little while he
sat.

Ostensibly he was reading manuscripts,
several of which lay on the table ; really he

was looking about him in a listless, idle, contented sort of mood.

The bookcase with its glass doors and well-filled shelves ; the thick carpet, worn a little round the table and where the feet of anxious and hopeful, and despairing and successful, and well-to-do and impecunious authors had trodden ; the bust of Socrates, mellowed by time and smoke ; the picture, hanging in a bad light, which Mr. Vassett had picked up a bargain in Drury Lane, and still believed to be an old master and priceless, though he could find no one else to share his opinion ; the quaint chimney-piece and the round mirror above it—placed, fortunately, too high to reflect the distorted face of any human being ; the library-table, on which so many letters had been written and cheques signed ; the small cabinet, where were dozens of manuscripts kept till the proper time came for returning them to their owners ; the window, the lower panes of which were cunningly ornamented with various curious designs intended to prevent a too close scrutiny of the back regions—all these things and many more had been familiar to Mr. Pierson for years, yet they now seemed to strike him with a quite fresh sense of pleasure and novelty, and to inspire the feeling that in so comfortable and home-like a room it would be a pity to exhaust his mind by doing anything.

'Bad as the weather is,' considered Mr. Pierson, 'they'll be coming in after a while. It is of no use beginning anything. I'll just lie on my oars for a little;' and, having so decided, he threw himself into Mr. Vassett's easy-chair, stretched his legs out over the hearthrug, and, basking in the heat of an immense fire, began to think, amongst other things and people, about Lady Hilda Hicks.

'I wonder she doesn't come. I made quite sure we should have seen her ere now,' he thought. 'What can she be doing? We may be certain of one thing, at any rate, namely, that where-ever she is she is up to no good;' and he gazed into the fire dreamily as his thoughts wandered off to the affairs of Mr. Hicks and his wife, and his hopes that he should make something out of the settlement of the matrimonial squabble.

There are things understood which are never exactly spoken, and Mr. Pierson knew Mr. Daunt would write him a cheque if he was able to carry out what he had promised to undertake.

' He will " recognise" my part in the transaction, to adopt Vassett's favourite expression,' thought the reader, ' and I certainly do not consider he can do that properly under twenty pounds. How shall I spend twenty pounds when I get the cheque? It is a long time since I had twenty pounds of my own in my hand at once.'

There were persons who pitied Mr. Pierson, who thought what a sad thing it was for a man possessed of his intellect—so well educated, so clever, so industrious, so honest, so assiduous—to be forced by cruel circumstances to fill a subordinate position. Mr. Vassett himself had once been of this opinion, and really hesitated about offering him the vacant post in Craven Street ; but he knew Mr. Pierson better now, and if he did not exactly comprehend why he had never got on, he grasped the fact that his reader never would get on.

There were two qualities, amongst many, Mr. Pierson lacked—ambition and self-denial. If he desired a thing to-day, and found himself possessed of enough money to purchase it, he would purchase, no matter what he went without to-morrow : and as he loved his ease more than power, or position, or social standing, the prize could not have been offered which would have induced steady application on his part.

By starts he was industrious and energetic ; but as a rule he had to be driven to read manuscripts and answer letters and return proofs.

Had it not been for this quality he might have risen high in a good house—eventually, perhaps, become partner in it to a small extent ; but there came a time when even his abilities could not counterbalance his sins of dilatoriness and omission, and he and the great publishing firm referred to parted company not on the best of terms.

It was then Mr. Vassett, who had been acquainted with Mr. Pierson slightly for years, met him lounging aimlessly along Piccadilly, and stopped to speak.

Mr. Pierson was full of his wrongs—and, as the other side of the case did not chance to be represented, he made out a very full bill of complaint.

He rehearsed all he had done for the firm,

and did not hide his own light under a bushel. He mentioned all the many great writers who, coming to his principals poor and unknown, would have been sent empty away but for his prescience. He dwelt upon the manner he had 'worked up' a certain magazine when the editor walked off in a huff, taking his staff with him. He declared he had been treated with the vilest ingratitude. He expressed his belief that the elder partners, though they had got of late 'mighty uppish' and hard to endure would never have parted in the manner they did with so old and faithful a servant, but for the machinations of a certain 'young puppy' lately admitted into the business.

'And what are you doing now?' asked Mr. Vassett, with a sincere feeling of sympathy; for, as was natural, he did not love the great firm with that affection brother publishers should entertain for each other. 'What are you doing now?'

'Starving,' answered Mr. Pierson.

It was not quite true, but it served. Mr. Vassett knew that it was easy for a man who has not saved, soon to feel the iron grip of actual want. He felt very sorry indeed for

25—2

Mr. Pierson, whom hitherto he had always seen well dressed and apparently well cared for. He knew large houses are not, as a rule, too considerate. He was aware that the ways and manners and habits of 'young puppies' are often trying to those over whom they chance to be placed in authority ; it hurt him to see a 'man like Pierson' with a frayed shirt-collar and a coat very white at the seams ; so he said :

'Mine is a small business after that you have been accustomed to ; but still it has grown a little too large for me ; therefore, if you care to come to Craven Street till something more suitable offers, I dare say we can agree about terms.'

Mr. Pierson jumped at the proposal, and declaring that he had no doubt they could, volunteered to 'look in' the next afternoon.

Thus he came, and thus he stayed. The business exactly suited him ; if he liked to absent himself for a day, or even two, Mr. Vassett made no complaint ; if he chose to let the manuscripts accumulate for a week, the publisher was not—to quote his own expression —'after him tooth and nail.' So far as he

could like anyone—which was not far—he
liked his employer; he would have felt extremely sorry had Mr. Vassett failed or died,
for he knew he would not drop into such
another berth; he had as little to do as the
heart of man could desire, and that little he
did at his own time and in his own way. Mr.
Vassett treated him not only as an equal, but
as a friend. He was not kept at arm's length
in Craven Street, as he had been in Golden
Square. He knew all the ins and outs of
every transaction; he was shown the letters;
he was consulted in difficulties; he was remembered in success; and, in a word, Mr.
Vassett, without making any fuss or display
about the matter, did to Mr. Pierson as he
would that others should have done by him
had he been in a similar worldly position, and
if an attached and devoted adherence did not
prove the result, it was merely because Mr.
Pierson was utterly deficient both in attach-
ment and devotion. He had not cared for father
or mother, brother or sister—he did not care
for wife or children; and, therefore, it is not
to be wondered at that he did not spend his
days thinking how he might best exhibit deep

gratitude for all Mr. Vassett's kindness to him.

He was faithful to the best of his ability, and if that ability was not of the most trustworthy order, Mr. Vassett did not expect to find perfection even in the person of a reader; so the two got on together very well indeed.

At an early stage of their business connection an arrangement had, with the concurrence of Mr. Pierson, been entered into between Mr. Vassett and Mrs. Pierson—namely, that a certain sum was to be 'kept back' each week in order that the rent might be duly provided for as each quarter came round.

'That's all I wants from him,' exclaimed Mrs. Pierson, who, as Mr. Vassett mildly put it, 'was not a highly educated person.'

At that period he pitied Mr. Pierson most heartily for having so thrown himself away, but he learned in the course of time the pity was due to the wife.

'It is a very strange world,' Mr. Vassett was wont to remark, and in this conclusion no doubt Mrs. Pierson would have agreed with the publisher most fully.

That Mr. Pierson much preferred Mr. Vas-

sett's house to his own is as little doubtful as
that Mrs. Pierson always felt thankful when
her husband was out of the way. For this
reason it was Mr. Pierson made long hours at
Craven Street; often stopping to take tea
with his employer, and not slipping on his out-
of-door coat so as to be ready to start when
the first stroke of the clock indicated that the
time for leaving business had come, as is too
much the habit with old and young gentlemen
on salaries at the present day.

The reader was still exercising the powers of
his mind, not in deciding upon the merits of
any particular manuscript, but in speculating
concerning the probable amount of the cheque
he saw, in anticipation, signed and cashed,
when the clerk who reigned supreme in the
outer office—who attended to the book-keeping,
kept bores civilly at bay, supplied the wants
of collectors who then, as now, went about
with heavy loads on their shoulders, and
grumbled a good deal when they could not
instantly get what they wanted, and always
seemed to be sent out in the worst weather
possible, and were afflicted with chronic
coughs, and indulged in a good deal of ' chaff'

—opened the door and announced that a lady wanted to see Mr. Vassett.

'Well, he's ill, you know,' answered Mr. Pierson.

'Will you see her then?' asked the other with a sad want of respect, born perhaps of knowing more of Mr. Pierson even than his master did. 'She has never been here before,' he added in explanation.

'What is she like?' inquired the reader.

'She is just like the rest of them,' returned the clerk, in whose breast familiarity with the aspect of 'rising talent' had bred something very near akin to contempt.

'Show her in, then,' said Mr. Pierson, resignedly murmuring as he turned to the table and began turning over the manuscripts. 'I must some day get Muggins to tell me "what they are all like."'

The lady entered. Though she had just come in from the wet street she looked trim and spruce enough to have stepped that moment out of a band-box.

Her hair was not dishevelled; her bonnet was straight, the strings tied in an admirable bow. On her skirts there was no speck of mud; her boots were not splashed; her manner was calm and self-possessed. It might have been quite a beautiful day in summer for all the signs of distress she exhibited.

'What a dreadful person to live with!' thought Mr. Pierson; but he only remarked audibly, whilst with a solemn dignity worthy of Mr. Vassett himself he indicated a chair, 'that the weather was most unpleasant.'

'It is not very agreeable, certainly,' said the lady, with admirable composure; 'but at least it has this advantage—one finds every person is at home.'

Mr. Pierson did not compromise himself by making any reply, and his visitor proceeded:

'It is such an absolute waste of time calling at different places and finding no one within able to give a definite answer on any subject.'

Still Mr. Pierson did not speak; there were times when he was fond of thus playing a waiting game, and on such occasions he proved himself an absolute master of the art of silence. By experience he knew nothing brings a woman so soon to the point as making no comment on what she says; and having taken a dislike to his visitor, he thought he would get her to the point as soon as possible.

The result proved his wisdom, for in her very next sentence she broke ground.

'I sent a manuscript to you a fortnight ago,' she said, 'with a note requesting you to give me a speedy answer. As yet I have received no reply.'

'I am sorry for that,' observed Mr. Pierson, in a manner that might have been taken either as ironical or sympathetic, as his auditor chose to interpret his tone.

'Oh, I did not much expect an answer,' she proceeded. 'I am told that you never take the slightest notice of letters.'

'Your informant must have some curious ideas as to the mode in which we conduct our business,' remarked Mr. Pierson, with unruffled serenity.

'I did not mean you in particular. I mean all publishers.'

'I assure you, madam, we reply to letters,' protested Mr. Pierson.

'Then why did you not reply to mine?'

'That I am quite unable to inform you,' he answered. 'A fortnight, however, is not a long time to give. If you only saw the number of manuscripts which arrive each morning, instead of wondering at a slight delay, you would marvel they so soon receive consideration.'

' I do not think I should,' she retorted. 'But however, to leave the general and come to the particular question, have you looked at the papers I sent you ?'

' If you will kindly tell me what they were, I may be able to say. I am still, remember, ignorant even of your name.'

' My name is Yarlow—*Miss* Yarlow,' she added, with emphasis—('As if,' thought Mr. Pierson, ' any human being could imagine you were a married woman !')—'but as I do not wish it to be published, I attached a *nom de plume* to the manuscript.'

' And what was the nature of the manuscript?' asked Mr. Pierson.

' Well, it was an attempt to reproduce in popular and attractive form the life stories of six French actresses. Such subjects, even when treated in a more prolix style, have generally been found to possess a great interest for the mass of readers, and I am assured by good judges that these biographies, dealt with

as I have done, only require to be well placed
before the public to secure a wide audience.
My knowledge of French literature is quite
exceptional, and my information has been
drawn from sources, I have reason to believe,
inaccessible to any other author.'

'I fear, however,' ventured Mr. Pierson,
'that the time for these sort of compilations
has rather gone by.'

'Compilations!' repeated the lady; 'my
manuscript is original—every word of it.'

'Then it can't contain the biographies of
six French actresses, or even one of them,'
objected the reader.

'It is perfectly evident you have not read a
line it contains,' said the author.

'I have not, certainly; but I do not see
how that fact can alter my contention.'

'Has anyone looked through the work?'
asked Miss Yarlow indignantly.

'That is a question you ought to be able to
answer much better than I,' replied Mr. Pierson. 'You alone can tell how many publishers
have seen the manuscript, and you alone can
judge, from the nature of their comments, how
many have read it through.'

Miss Yarlow, though not much given to blushing, coloured up to her eyes. He had struck her in a vital part at last. There was not a publisher in London of any standing to whom she had not offered those memoirs, and there was not a publisher of any standing in London who had not refused to have anything to do with them. Quite unconsciously, she and Miss Westley had been traversing the same round, with the same result. Glenarva happened to have 'worked the trade' more exhaustively; but that only chanced because she was younger, ignorant of many conventionalities which bound and fettered Miss Yarlow, and less careful of herself altogether than that personally considerate lady.

'I wonder of what use publishers really are!' said Miss Yarlow, at last recovering from the cruel blow Mr. Pierson had dealt her. She did not address this pleasing remark to him, but uttered it in a sort of involuntary soliloquy, the expression of feeling being wrung from her by actual stress of despair.

'I really cannot inform you,' answered Mr. Pierson, though he knew she had not spoken to him. 'Probably, however, they are in-

tended to serve some purpose—whether good
or evil it is not for me to say—in the scheme
of creation.'

Miss Yarlow looked at him.   She looked for
a moment as if she were at bay—as if she
would have liked to cross over to where he
sat and box his ears or pull his hair ; then,
apparently feeling how useless it was to fight
against a power such as that he possessed, she
said, in a more humble and conciliatory
manner than she had yet employed :

'And you—you, I suppose, like the rest,
have not deigned to cast a glance on my poor
attempt ?'

'I have seen the manuscript—that is about
all ; but if it is likely to prove any satisfaction
to you, I will have it read now.   I fear, however, whatever its merits may be, you would
stand no chance of persuading Mr. Vassett to
undertake the publication at present.   His
lists are quite full for the season.'

'And when do you suppose——' faltered
Miss Yarlow.

'Next year, perhaps, he might be open to
consider a work of the kind you indicate.   I
beg your pardon, did you speak——'

'No, I did not speak,' answered Miss Yarlow ; and she sat and looked in dumb misery at the leaping firelight. Next year ! Gracious heavens ! Were years, she thought, so plentiful in a human life that any person could afford to waste one in waiting ?

'A year is a long time,' she said at last.

'To look forward to,' suggested Mr. Pierson.

'And you really will not help me ?'

'I really cannot help you,' he amended.

'And I heard Mr. Vassett was so exceptionally kind and courteous.'

'He is exceptionally kind and courteous,' argued Mr. Pierson, taking no notice of the suggested comparison implied as regarded himself ; 'but though he might frame his refusal more pleasantly than I have done, he would refuse all the same.'

'I wish I could have seen him,' she said.

'If he gets better you will, no doubt, be able to see him some time during the course of the spring.'

Miss Yarlow looked at the speaker as he unfolded this hopeful prospect in such a way that he felt compelled to add, 'But when you have seen him, I do not think you will find yourself much further forward.'

She did not reply. She only turned her eyes again towards the fire.

'Does she mean to stop till we accept her manuscript?' marvelled Mr. Pierson. He had seen a great many authors and a great many women, but he had never before come across any author or any woman exactly resembling Miss Yarlow. He was beginning to wonder when she would go—what he should be obliged to do to get rid of her—when the door opened, and Muggins appeared to say: 'Mr. Dawton has been waiting for some time. He wishes to know if he shall call as he returns from Fleet Street.'

'No, no,' interrupted Mr. Pierson hurriedly; 'ask him to stop a few moments longer. I want to see him particularly. Give him the *Morning Post* to look at.'

'He has read it through, sir,' explained Muggins, who took in the position at a glance.

'Well, say I shall be disengaged directly. Have you tried any of the magazines?' asked Mr. Pierson, turning to Miss Yarlow as Muggins withdrew.

'No,' she answered, still looking intently at the fire.

'I think you might find it worth your while to do so.'

'Probably their lists would be full also,' remarked Miss Yarlow, with a fine irony.

There ensued a dead silence, which Mr. Pierson at length essayed to break by rising from his chair and making a feint of arranging the papers scattered on the table; but Miss Yarlow took not the slightest notice of this movement.

Was she going to beat him with his own weapons? Was he at last to find that saying nothing may, on the part of a woman, be even more of a vice than a virtue?

'The best counsel I can offer you,' he began, when he felt he could endure her rapt contemplation of the fire no longer, 'is to try the magazines. Even if editors should consider your articles unsuitable, you would be in no worse position than you are now; while if by any good chance you did secure acceptance, papers of the description you indicate would be just as available for publication after they had appeared in a periodical as they are now.'

Miss Yarlow removed her eyes from the leaping flames, and looked at Mr. Pierson with considerable interest. Clearly here was a lady who, though she could be dumb, did not happen to be deaf.

' I think you really will find that your best plan,' went on Mr. Pierson, anxious to follow up the impression he had made. ' If you do not know where the offices of the leading magazines are situated, I will write you down the addresses with pleasure.'

Coming from the source it did, this offer should have been regarded as extremely courteous ; but Miss Yarlow did not seem much impressed by it.

' Was there ever such a woman ?' thought Mr. Pierson impatiently. Instead of taking the blessings that the gods sent her, and going out into the rain rejoicing, with a few useless names and addresses written on them in a hand so clear as to convey a tacit reproof to careless caligraphers, Miss Yarlow simply took no notice whatever of the civility proffered, but, seizing upon the one point in Mr. Pierson's previous sentence which had seemed to her worthy of attention, asked :

'Do I understand you to mean that hereafter, whether these memoirs have appeared
in print or not, Mr. Vassett will entertain the
idea of publishing them ?'

' I scarcely intended to say he would " entertain the idea of publishing them," ' amended
Mr. Pierson, who felt he had to do with a lady
whom it might be inexpedient to mislead even
in the way of kindness, ' because so many ex-
traneous circumstances, entirely independent
of the merits of your productions, have to be
considered before a work by an as yet unknown author can be produced with satisfaction
to all parties concerned.'

' What did you intend to say, then ?' inquired the lady, with a directness which might
have elicited some tangible statement even
from Mr. Vassett, who had a peculiarly happy
knack of combining ambiguity with courtesy.

' That after your " Six French Actresses "
have appeared in a magazine we shall be as
happy to read and consider them as at the
present moment,' answered Mr. Pierson, driven
to bay, and not perceiving the mistake he had
made till reminded by a contemptuous ex-
clamation from Miss Yarlow of how very little

satisfaction his assurance was calculated to give.

'Well, you are a Jesuit!' remarked Miss Yarlow, irritation tempered by admiration struggling together in her tone for mastery. 'Why can't you tell me at once you never mean to read the manuscript? What is the good of all this beating about the bush?'

'You *will* misconceive me,' said Mr. Pierson desperately. "If it is likely to prove any satisfaction to you, the manuscript shall be read immediately; but I tell you candidly, that let the report turn out as favourable as report possibly can, there is not the slightest likelihood of Mr. Vassett accepting the work at present. He does not care to bring out many books; and his arrangements are made for some time to come. If the author of "Nine Poems by V.," or Charlotte Brontë, or even Miss Martineau herself, were to offer him a manuscript at the present moment, I know perfectly well he would say its appearance must be deferred, otherwise he should reluctantly be obliged to decline it.'

Oh, days that seem gone so long! When 'Jane Eyre' and 'Paul Ferroll' were titles as familiar in men's mouths as 'Lady Audley's Secret' and the 'Woman in White' have been since; when Miss Martineau was still living, and the 'Scenes of Clerical Life' were not thought of; when no one had heard of George Eliot, and publishers were still plodding slowly and safely along familiar roads; when all the world had not begun to write, and there were still left a small number of persons who read!

On that particularly wet morning those days now departed were present with Mr. Pierson, and the names he invoked to convince his visitor of the thorough honesty of his assertions stood high on the glory-roll of fame.

'Perhaps,' suggested Miss Yarlow, 'Mr. Vassett is waiting for the reappearance of the Queen of Sheba carrying a roll of manuscript in her hand containing an account of her visit to the court of King Solomon.'

'He may be,' answered Mr. Pierson coolly; 'but he has not mentioned the fact to me. And now, Miss Yarlow, to revert to your matter. Will you leave your " Six Actresses " to be read, or will you adopt my advice, and first submit them to one or other of the magazines ?'

'I think,' said the lady, 'as you are so evidently anxious to get rid of my manuscript and myself, I had better take it with me. The next time I come I hope Mr. Vassett will be well enough to attend to his business for himself.'

'It is gratifying to find there is at least one point on which we are agreed,' answered Mr. Pierson, as he opened the cabinet and took out the despised 'Actresses.'

'Mr. Dawton, sir,' here interrupted Muggins, opening the door—and never surely was the sight of Muggins' face more welcome— 'wishes to know if you could speak to him for one minute. He says he need not now detain you longer, but he has an appoint- ment——'

'Ask Mr. Dawton to walk in,' said Mr. Pierson ; 'and, see, Muggins, put up this manuscript. Can we send it anywhere for you ?' he asked, turning to Miss Yarlow.

'No, thank you,' answered that lady.

'We will with pleasure,' urged Mr. Pierson ; 'it is a bulky parcel for you to take.'

'A workman should not be above carrying his tools,' said Miss Yarlow, with a beautiful humility.

'Good! Excellent!' exclaimed a voice behind her; and, turning, she beheld a most singular - looking person, who bowed and smiled, and hoped she would 'excuse an old man's appreciation of her ready wit.'

It was Mr. Dawton. Mr. Dawton dressed as if it were a hot July afternoon—in grey trousers, a white waistcoat, a swallow-tailed coat, a washing necktie. The only item inconsistent, perhaps, with the idea of sultry weather was a pair of Hessian boots; but the boots were beautifully made and highly polished, and detracted in no way from the astounding effect of the general get-up.

'Why, Dawton!' exclaimed Mr. Pierson, 'where are you going? What have you been doing? Getting married this fine sunshiny morning, eh?'

'No, my friend; I married once—more years ago than I can remember.'

'And found it once too often, eh?'

'Not so. My draw in the matrimonial lottery proved singularly fortunate. Let who

else will—but we must not talk treason in the
presence of so fair a representative of her sex,'
Mr. Dawton broke off to say, with a winning
smile, and his hand laid on his heart : '*Are
you going, madam ?* I trust my appearance
was not inopportune ?'

'You had better put that question to Mr.
Pierson,' answered Miss Yarlow, with a Par-
thian glance shot at that gentleman ; and
then, announcing her intention of waiting in
the outer office till Muggins had finished tying
up her manuscript, she bade her late adversary
good-morning, and walked out of the inner
room, followed by a look of profound admiration from Mr. Dawton, to whom she bowed
stiffly, and who held the door wide and
watched her retreating figure as he might have
done had she been retiring down one of the
" wings " from the gaze of thousands.

'Ah !' he exclaimed, as he reluctantly closed
the portal between him and this vision of
loveliness, ' there's nothing like woman.'

'That depends a good deal, I should say, on
what the woman is,' returned Mr. Pierson,
drawing a deep sigh of relief. 'Well, and
what can I do for you ?' he added, motioning

to the chair Miss Yarlow had just vacated, and
flinging himself into the depths of the sacred
armchair.

'Vassett's laid up, your clerk tells me,'
observed Mr. Dawton, sitting well on the edge
of his seat, and holding his hat in his hand,
after the most approved traditions of how a
gentleman (on the stage) comports himself
when paying a morning visit.

Mr. Pierson inclined his head in indolent
acquiescence.

'Nothing serious the matter, I trust?'

'No—a cold—this beastly weather has been
too much for him; for beastly weather it is,
though you are arrayed as if the young lambs
were frisking about in the green meadows,
and you were intending to join their gambols.'

'You think I really look the character,
then?'

'What character, in the name of Heaven?'
asked Mr. Pierson.

'The country squire—the good old country
gentleman of ancient lineage, and possessed of
broad acres, antiquated and prejudiced it may
be, but true to his principles. Conservative
even in his dress—up in town to see a friend

at court, with a view of obtaining a lucrative
appointment abroad for his prodigal son. His
appearance tells its own story. If you were
to meet him in an omnibus now——'

'I should think, if I met you in an
omnibus, dressed as you are now, you had
either escaped from Bedlam, or were a fit
candidate for it.'

'Ah! I see you don't understand——'

'The fun of a man at your time of life turning out on such a morning in a white waistcoat and a frilled shirt—no, faith, I can't
understand that. However, if the costume
pleases you, I am sure it may please me.'

'Wait a bit, my boy—fair and softly wins
the day—wait till I send you tickets.'

'Oh, it is a play, then? I thought as
much! But you are not going to perform in
Craven Street? Why the deuce do you
choose to roam about the town with no
clothing on your back to speak of?'

'I attribute most of the success I have
achieved in my life—and mine, Pierson, has
been an eventful life—— By-the-bye,' Mr.
Dawton broke off to say, 'I suppose you
have read the manuscript I sent here some

short time since, containing just a few jottings of an experience which has not been unexciting?

'I only looked at a page or two; Mr. Vassett read it.'

'And what did you think of it — now, candidly?'

'I thought it very poor stuff indeed,' answered Mr. Pierson, with a frankness which could be considered as nothing less than appalling, 'but Vassett imagines something can be done with it.'

'You see, you are scarcely a judge of matters connected with the noble profession,' said Mr. Dawton, much as if he merely substituted this sentence for — 'You see, you are only an ignorant fool.'

'No; I do not profess to know much about the stage, but I fancy I comprehend something about literature.'

'Ah! I sent the sheets to you in the rough; they require a little correction, I am aware—a mere matter of detail,' said Mr. Dawton.

'And who is going to undertake that correction?' asked Mr. Pierson, who certainly did not desire to undertake it himself.

'Well, as you know, I have sons—all capable,

all good men and true. The mere preparation
for press need present no difficulty. I should
have liked to see Mr. Vassett,' proceeded Mr.
Dawton, with a wandering expression in his
eyes and a furtive glance, the meaning of which
Mr. Pierson could read perfectly, 'because I
want the work brought out soon—now, in fact,
when all London will be ringing with my name
—and you and I could not settle terms, I suppose?'

'No, certainly not,' answered Mr. Pierson,
with a prompt acquiescence which proved anything but gratifying to Mr. Dawton.

'I wish I could have seen Mr. Vassett,' he
said, as if he had not made the same statement
before.

'Well, I have little doubt he will be able to
attend to business in a few days.'

'Ah! but I wanted to see him this day'—
which fact he need not indeed have told Mr.
Pierson, who comprehended thoroughly not
merely that he wanted to see Mr. Vassett, but
also why he wanted to see him.

There was a pause. Mr. Pierson stirred the
fire, and Mr. Dawton looked at the blaze almost
as intently as Miss Yarlow had done.

'Well, they *are* a queer set !' considered Mr. Pierson, referring, like Mr. Muggins, to authors in general, and forgetting how extremely odd he himself could be on occasion. 'I wonder how long it will be before *he* speaks ?'

It was not long—silence could not be reckoned amongst Mr. Dawton's failings.

'Do you think,' he began in a subdued and confidential tone, 'Mr. Vassett is so ill that reading a note—a very short note—would hurt him ?'

'I don't suppose it would,' answered Mr. Pierson ; but he spoke doubtfully, and not at all as a man might have been expected to speak who knew perfectly well his principal was able to come downstairs to attend to his business had it pleased him to do so. 'Should you like to write him a note ?'

'Thank you. Yes, I should ;' and Mr. Dawton laid his hat down carefully, drew his chair to the table, accepted with a bland inclination of his head the paper Mr. Pierson placed before him, and took pen in hand, as he might have done had the eyes of pit, stalls, boxes, and gallery been concentrated upon his act.

Never a man existed so utterly permeated by his profession as poor Mr. Dawton. When he laid him down to sleep and drew the sheets up under his elderly chin, there can be no question he felt still before the footlights, and in his last conscious waking moments posed for the ' gods.'

Though he dipped the pen in the ink he did not write, however. He sat considering what he wanted to say, and how he had best say it ; then, probably finding the task more difficult than he expected, he said to Mr. Pierson :

' I do not think I need trouble Mr. Vassett with a note at all, if you would only be so kind as to take a message to him. Could you do this for me ?'

Mr. Pierson thought he could, but before fully committing himself, intimated it might be as well for him to know what the message was.

' Well, the fact is,' said Mr. Dawton, ' I have most unexpectedly and unaccountably forgotten to bring any money out with me, and there is something I wish particularly to pay this morning. If you explain the difficulty in which I am placed to Mr. Vassett, perhaps he would be so good as to advance me a nominal sum, say five pounds. I should feel infinitely obliged to him ; I really should—and to you also,' added Mr. Dawton as an afterthought.

'I will ask him with pleasure,' replied Mr. Pierson ; 'but of course I can't say whether he has any five-pound notes lying about,' with which depressing observation the reader disappeared, leaving Mr. Dawton to go through the charm, 'He will, he will not'—minus the 'property' flower.

Mr. Pierson was not long absent. He came back almost directly, and saying, 'Yes, you can have five pounds,' opened a drawer, from which he took Mr. Vassett's cheque-book.

Mr. Dawton tried hard to hide the relief he felt under the words,

'I am infinitely obliged to him,' uttered in a majestic tone and with a dignified composure; but Mr. Pierson saw his whole face change its fashion for a moment with delight, and laughed to himself as he went up the stairs with the cheque-book.

He had not reached the first landing, however, before his name was pronounced, and looking back, he beheld Mr. Dawton making mystical signs for him to return.

Mr. Pierson was the last man on earth to do anything of the sort unless he knew exactly what he was wanted for.

'One moment!' exclaimed Mr. Dawton.

'Yes,' said the reader, standing still.

'Not crossed,' entreated Mr. Dawton in a stage-whisper, putting his hand to the side of his mouth, so that no breath of his utterance might be wafted along the passage. 'Open.'

'All right,' answered Mr. Pierson ; and then Mr. Dawton walked back into the office on tiptoe, and as if there were mortal sickness in the house, to be suddenly confronted with an unexpected apparition, which addressed him sharply and imperatively with the words :

'Where's Mr. Pierson ?'

'Madam,' said Mr. Dawton, backing a step or two, for he felt really frightened, 'the gentleman will wait upon you directly.'

'He had better !' exclaimed the lady, walking round the table ; and flinging herself into Mr. Vassett's armchair, she commenced beating a tattoo on the floor with her little feet, which she made no scruple of freely exhibiting to Mr. Dawton.

'Will you—may I offer you the newspaper pending Mr. Pierson's return?' he asked, timidly extending the *Morning Post*, which he had brought in from the outer office.

'No,' she snapped, and beat a louder tattoo than before.

Mr. Dawton retreated as if he had got a slap in the face, and stood looking in surprise, not unmixed with terror, at this last specimen of 'angelic woman.'

'Now, is that man ever coming?' she cried, suddenly turning sharply round, and catching Mr. Dawton staring at her with more curiosity than good-breeding.

'I assure you, madam, he will be back almost immediately,' he stammered.

'Go and fetch him at once.'

If she had told him in that tone to take off his head, Mr. Dawton would have tried to obey her; and accordingly he again went out into the passage, where he ran up against Mr. Pierson, who had paused for a moment at sound of the well-known voice.

'Stormy weather impending,' he thought;

and then Mr. Dawton appeared as if he had
been blown out of the room, and said, with a
scared face and in a tremulous voice—'A lady
—a—a lady——'

'I know,' interrupted Mr. Pierson. 'Here's
your cheque—put it up. You did not let out
I was with Vassett, I hope, did you?'

'N—n—no,' answered Mr. Dawton, who at
the moment had not the slightest recollection
of anything he might have 'let out.' 'I have
left my hat in the room.'

'Come and get it then,' advised Mr. Pierson.
'Bless my soul, she won't eat you.'

'Take her for all in all——!' began Mr.
Dawton, but Mr. Pierson was by this time in
the room, and the storm had burst.

CHAPTER IV.

A QUARTER of an hour passed ; comparative calm had succeeded to tempest, and Mr. Pierson was still alive. There were times during that exceedingly bad fifteen minutes when he held his head in both hands to make sure it was still on his body. Like a hurricane, Lady Hilda's passion threatened to carry everything away before it. For once Mr. Dawton was stricken dumb ; in the outer office the usually phlegmatic Muggins stood listening, ready, as he afterwards stated, to ' make a clean bolt of it,' should flight become necessary. On the first floor, with door ajar, Mr. Vassett hearkened, appalled by her ladyship's torrent

27—2

of indignation, doubtful whether, in spite of anything Mr. Pierson might have said on the subject of his ailments, he ought not to descend to his reader's assistance. Prudence, however, overcame valour, and Mr. Vassett decided that upon the whole he had better let Pierson fight out the battle alone.

Bravely enough Mr. Pierson stood his ground; though her ladyship's balls were whistling round him, though he had to bear the brunt of a hot and heavy cannonade, his courage never really failed.

'It was bad while it lasted,' he remarked afterwards, ' and it lasted a long time.'

Nevertheless, spite of the fury and violence of the storm, he managed now and then to edge in a word. Notwithstanding the enemy's fire, he stood firm to his own guns.

' As Lady Hilda had altered her book, she need never expect to find any good publisher to stand godfather to it.' ' Her ladyship could, of course, if she doubted the fact, take it the round of the trade—to Longman, Chapman and Hall, Bentley, Hurst and Blackett, or any other firm she could think of.' ' He felt as satisfied as he could feel on any subject that she would not get a respectable house to put their imprint upon it.'

' Then I will get a house that is not respectable,' retorted her ladyship.

' I don't think you will,' answered Mr. Pierson, ' unless your husband proves willing to give a guarantee for damages.'

' Don't talk to me about my husband !' cried Lady Hilda, and then the storm, which had lulled for a moment, burst forth again.

But at last it really seemed as if the worst were over, as if her irate ladyship had exhausted her almost inexhaustible powers of speech. She saw, in fact, there was nothing to be done with Mr. Pierson ; and so, now flinging herself once again into Mr. Vassett's chair—she had stood during the controversy so as to give greater effort to her threats and denunciations—she said she meant to remain there till Mr. Vassett was produced.

' He undertook to bring out my novel,' she said, ' and I must hear from his own lips why he refuses to do so.'

' I am afraid your ladyship will have to wait some time, then,' said Mr. Pierson. ' Mr.

Vassett is very ill indeed. I fear he will not be able to come downstairs for some weeks.'

' If that is all,' answered Lady Hilda, ' I am quite able to go upstairs this minute ;' and she started from her seat, as if to carry her suggestion into immediate effect.

' Mr. Vassett is in bed,' explained Mr. Pierson, with reckless mendacity. ' You would not go to him there !'

' I would go to him if he were in his coffin, sir,' said Lady Hilda.

' Ah, that would be quite another affair !' remarked the reader, who could not have withheld his tongue from an observation of this sort if life itself had depended upon his silence.

Lady Hilda looked at him. Could a glance have killed, Mr. Pierson had never again returned home to his wife and family. Her eyes literally seemed to flash fire ; and as she stood there, erect and indignant, waiting, apparently, to swoop down and destroy her quarry, Mr. Dawton thought he beheld before him the very incarnation of a handsome virago.

The storm, which had seemed passing away,

now gave signs of working round again. The sky grew black, the atmosphere thick and heavy, and there appeared no likelihood of another thunderclap being averted, when, 'for the first time on any stage,' Mr. Dawton quite unconsciously played the part of 'special Providence.'

Hitherto he had failed to get his hat. Fearing to venture out into the open, and so draw Lady Hilda's attention to himself, he remained behind Mr. Pierson, and, under cover of that gentleman's body, made several futile attempts to secure his head-covering. Now, however, feeling satisfied another tempest was impending, which might prove even worse than any of its predecessors, he 'dodged' from side to side of Mr. Pierson in a manner which must have won the approval of his particular friends, the gods ; and all his eyes fastened on his hat, and his whole energies devoted to securing it, forgot for a moment the awful presence in which he stood.

Lady Hilda's attention was at last arrested by his gestures.

'What does that creature want ?' she asked Mr. Pierson sharply. 'Is he mad ?'

'No—your ladyship—no,' stammered out Mr. Dawton. 'I—I do not want to interrupt —I am sure—and I beg a thousand pardons— but——'

'What is it?' said Mr. Pierson, who had for some time been oblivious of his presence.

'He wants his hat. Can't you see?'

And snatching up the extremely shiny article in question, Lady Hilda was 'graciously' pleased to thrust it towards Mr. Dawton in the most rude and ungracious manner possible.

'I beg your pardon, I am sure,' apologized Mr. Pierson; 'I had quite forgotten. This is a gentleman, Lady Hilda,' he added, thankful for even a moment's diversion, 'with whose name I have no doubt you are well acquainted——'

Lady Hilda looked at the actor curiously, as she might at a chameleon, or a prairie dog, or a kangaroo, or any other animal she did not know familiarly.

He now came forward a step, as if to the footlights, and, laying his hand on his white waistcoat, and bowing profoundly, murmured :

'Dawton—Dawton, at your ladyship's service.'

'What's his name?' demanded Lady Hilda, turning to Mr. Pierson.

'Dawton,' said the reader.

'Never heard it before,' observed her ladyship, with contemptuous brevity.

'A mere tyro in the arena where your ladyship has won renown,' explained Mr. Dawton, who had not the faintest idea even of her ladyship's lawful name. 'The few laurel leaves I have been permitted to gather,' he added, touching his forehead, which was adorned at that moment by a perfectly new wig, 'have been culled by me in Thespian groves. On the mimic stage the name of Dawton has achieved distinction — three generations have trodden the boards, and left, if I may so express myself, an imprint on the sands behind them. I have sons who will, I think—in literature, in art, in the drama—keep up the old traditions; and, for myself, I am your ladyship's most humble and admiring servant.'

Lady Hilda laughed — actually laughed. Like Mr. Donagh, she had a keen sense of humour when the joke was not at her own expense ; and the spectacle of Mr. Dawton, dressed as he was and acting for the benefit of herself and Mr. Pierson, might indeed have moved the mirth of Muggins, who in the outer office heard Lady Hilda's laugh, and wondered ' how Pierson had managed to bring her to at last.'

' This is delicious,' she remarked, turning to Mr. Pierson as the only appreciative individual within reach ; and then she smiled sweetly on Mr. Dawton, who, thawing under the influence of this unlooked-for condescension, proceeded :

' It is in the field of fiction, as I understand, your ladyship's proudest triumphs have been achieved ; and yet, if without impertinence I— who do possess some knowledge of that which is, after all, the noblest profession of all, the living, breathing, moving presentment of our actual existence—may venture such an observation, I feel confident that could your ladyship only be induced to represent before an audience the indignation—righteous indignation, I doubt not—it has been my privilege to hear you enunciate in this room, you would

bring down the house. No, I never in all my
long experience heard anything so magnificent. Siddons herself could not have done it,
madam.'

'Because Siddons had never such cause for
righteous anger,' answered Lady Hilda. 'I
don't know, Mr. Dawton—that is your name,
is it not?—what sort of treatment you may
meet with here, but I can only say Mr.
Vassett treats me shamefully. He keeps me
without money, and he desires also to prevent
my becoming famous. I have written a novel
—oh, such a novel!—one that must cause a
perfect furore, and now he says quite coolly—
or rather, Mr. Pierson says so for him—he
won't publish the book unless I cut out all
the finest passages, and reduce it to the dull
level of propriety and stupidity old ladies of
both sexes have set up as the standard of
literary perfection.'

Poor Mr. Dawton! With Mr. Vassett's
cheque in his pocket, with the hope of more
cheques from Mr. Vassett in his heart, he felt
the publisher's side of the question was that
he ought to espouse; the cause of propriety,
even if propriety involved stupidity, the

safest for him to champion. But, upon the other hand, he was at close quarters with a beautiful termagant, with 'angelic woman' in one of her most stormy moods, with a lady (of title) who seemed capable of doing anything if crossed, and yet who, in Mr. Dawton's then opinion, only required, like all the rest of her charming sex, a little discreet management to be delightful.

For the latter reason, and also because Mr. Vassett was absent and Lady Hilda present, with a deprecating glance towards Mr. Pierson, and feeling, as he pathetically put the matter subsequently, as Naaman after he was cured of his leprosy must when he bowed himself in the house of Rimmon, Mr. Dawton declared her ladyship had good reason for complaint; that if any passages were excised from his poor book, he should feel the operation acutely. But he was certain there must be some mistake. The matter only required explanation, and Mr. Vassett would see it was put right at once.

'I have had the pleasure of Mr. Vassett's acquaintance for over twenty years,' he said, 'and during the whole of that time I have

never known him to do an ungentlemanly
or ungenerous action. Besides, he could
not treat your ladyship's slightest wish with
discourtesy; he is kindness itself, most gal-
lant——'

At this point Mr. Pierson interrupted the
proceedings.

'Dawton,' he suggested, ' don't you want to
go to Fleet Street ?'

'Yes, certainly. I have an appointment
there.'

' Then hadn't you better keep it ?'

Mr. Dawton coloured up to the roots of his
wig; but he had not lived his life, even such
as it was, for nothing. Though Mr. Pierson's
lack of politeness, as he told the reader afterwards, ' entered into his very soul,' he turned
with a very good affectation of indifference to
Lady Hilda, observing, ' There is scant ceremony amongst friends, your ladyship will
perceive,' bowed profoundly to her, and saying, ' Good-morning, Pierson,' in a tone of hurt
dignity to that gentleman, retired from the
scene.

' Thank heaven,' observed Lady Hilda
piously, as the door closed behind him,

'one bore is disposed of! Well, Mr. Pierson?'

' Well, Lady Hilda?'

'Is it to be peace or war?'

'So far as I am concerned, peace always towards your ladyship; but you are aware I have a duty towards my employer also.'

'Fiddle-de-de!'

'And he has a duty to discharge towards himself.'

'Meaning he won't publish my book?'

'Meaning he cannot publish your book as it stands.'

'Then I must take it elsewhere; and I have been *so* ill, Mr. Pierson. I went to stay with a friend in the country for a few days, and got laid up there, and it was such a horrid house! And then, when I came back to town, expecting to find the book finished—no proofs, no letters, no anything! I wrote to the printers at once; they referred me to Mr. Vassett. I went to the printers; they referred me once again to Mr. Vassett. Now I come here, and I can't see Mr. Vassett, who I believe is keeping out of the way. I feel quite satisfied he is afraid or ashamed to meet me.'

'Whatever shame there may be in the matter,' said Mr. Pierson boldly, 'certainly does not attach itself to Mr. Vassett. To be quite plain, Lady Hilda, you tried to play him a most shabby trick, and one which, had it succeeded, might have proved his ruin as a publisher.'

'But why? Everyone would have read the book!'

'And said any man capable of sending out such a work was not fit to remain in the trade.'

'Oh! of course it is your interest to take his part.'

'There is such a thing in the world as honesty, though you, Lady Hilda. do not seem to believe in its existence,' remarked Mr. Pierson in a tone of conscious virtue.

'I do not think there is any audience,' suggested her sceptical ladyship, 'and moral sentiments of all kinds are quite thrown away upon me.'

'Indeed, I should imagine so,' replied the reader with disconcerting readiness.

'I wish I had never heard the name of Vassett!' exclaimed Lady Hilda. 'If I had only in the first instance gone to some good publisher, I might have been a rich woman by this time.'

'It is not too late for you to take this book to a good publisher.'

'And how in the world could I account for the novel being in print ?'

Mr. Pierson laughed outright as he answered :

'I should not presume to suggest to Lady Hilda Hicks the particular excuse it might seem most expedient to make use of. Your ladyship's vivid imagination may be trusted to find some way out of the difficulty.'

She did not speak for a moment ; but then she broke out again with this plaint :

'And I never in all my life wanted money so much—wanted it so cruelly.'

'If you had dealt fairly by Mr. Vassett, you need not have wanted money,' returned Mr. Pierson, who was getting too tired of the discussion to waste his breath in what he called 'figures of speech.'

'And till I can find an accommodating and sensible publisher, I shall not be able to get a penny, I suppose ?'

'I really do not know. Mr. Vassett will not advance even that small sum, I am very sure.'

'Come now, Mr. Pierson, could you not persuade him to bring out my book as it stands ?'

'I could not if I would, and I would not if I could,' answered Mr. Pierson, who was becoming quite disagreeable in the strength of his rectitude.

'There is really not an atom of harm in anything I have written,' she persisted.

'We will not travel over all that ground again, if you please, Lady Hilda.'

'All I wanted was to shame my husband into making me some decent allowance.'

Mr. Pierson maintained a discreet silence.

'I am quite sure you could not guess the pittance he has the conscience, or rather the want of conscience, to dole out to his wife.'

'Your ladyship mentioned the amount when you first came here,' answered Mr. Pierson. 'Six hundred per annum. I remember at the time thinking it was not actual starvation.'

'Perhaps it might not be to you.'

'Perhaps it might not be to a great many people,' answered the reader.

'But to me such a sum means absolute penury. And what makes the matter all the worse is the knowledge that twelve hundred a year would be no more to Mr. Hicks than—than what shall I say?'

'Twelve pence to me,' supplied Mr. Pierson.

'Thank you; I do not know that I could find a better simile.'

And Lady Hilda smiled sweetly, as if she had paid Mr. Pierson's pecuniary position some delicate compliment.

'Yes, I believe he is enormously rich,' said the reader, twisting and untwisting a piece of paper as he spoke. 'I wonder how people get to be so rich. Somebody was saying the other day Mr. Hicks had bought an estate, and paid—how much down for it?—quarter of a million, I fancy—yes, I think it was a quarter of a million.'

Lady Hilda leaned forward and listened with parted lips and eager eyes. He had interested her at last.

' Where is the estate ?' she asked.

' Let me see, did I hear ?—I must have done — Stifford ? Enfield ? Dulwich ? — no ; where on earth was it ? What's the place out somewhere to the north of London—not Hornsey, or Highgate ; Southgate—that's it, Southgate.'

' The property that belonged to the Dundas family—do you mean that ?'

Mr. Pierson shook his head, and contrived to look as if the subject had not contained the smallest interest for him.

' Some big man owned the place,' he said ; ' that is about all I know, except—yes, by-the-bye, I was nearly forgetting the most important part of the business—the person who told Mr. Vassett said it was currently reported Mr. Hicks meant to entertain Royalty this summer.'

Lady Hilda jumped straight off her chair, and then sat down again.

' And pray,' she asked, ' who is going to do the honours of this new house for Mr. Hicks when he receives Royalty ?'

' I can't say, I am sure. He has a sister, hasn't he ? I feel almost positive I heard some-

28—2

thing about a sister in connection with the matter.'

If Mr. Dawton had seen her ladyship then, he might have found something to say about 'bringing down the house.' A look which contained volumes swept over her expressive face. She did not speak, but Mr. Pierson understood. There was no need of words to tell him the strife which had raged between husband and wife was as nothing in comparison to the war Lady Hilda felt she could undertake against her sister-in-law.

At last Mr. Hicks's better-half broke the silence.

'That book *must* be published,' was her remark. '*She* is in it.'

Mr. Pierson raised his eyebrows and shrugged his shoulders.

'I really do not think,' he said, 'a publisher of any standing could be found to bring out your novel ; and this I know, that nothing would induce Mr. Vassett to do so.'

'Oh ! that I clearly understand,' snapped back Lady Hilda.

There ensued another pause, which Mr. Pierson suddenly ended by unexpectedly throwing out this remark : ' I suppose your settlements are all right ?'

Lady Hilda looked at him in amazement.

' What do you mean ?' she asked.

' But of course they are,' continued Mr. Pierson, as if answering some doubt raised by himself, ' considering the nature of the policy which has been pursued.'

' I do not understand. What are you talking about ?' cried Lady Hilda. ' Of course he is bound to pay me six hundred a year.'

' I was not thinking of that,' answered Mr. Pierson ; but he refrained from saying what he was thinking of.

' I wish you would explain !' exclaimed Lady Hilda irritably. ' You and Mr. Vassett are both so extremely fond of dark utterances.'

' I am not fond of dark utterances,' said Mr. Pierson deprecatingly, ' but I am equally averse to giving unnecessary offence. It was foolish of me to speak ; only, as the idea crossed my mind, I gave expression to it without due consideration.'

' Evidently you wish to drive me mad,' she returned. ' Tell me instantly what your idea was. I insist upon knowing.'

'You must not be angry with me, then,' he
pleaded; 'I admit it was a very silly notion,
but it came into my head without rhyme or
reason. What I thought of was this : I wondered if you were quite independent of Mr.
Hicks, and then I knew of course you must
be, or you would try to conciliate him a
little.'

'I am independent of him so far as that
wretched six hundred a year goes.'

'But was no other settlement made than
that ?'

'I don't know what you mean.'

'Was no settlement made before your
marriage ?'

'No ; there ought to have been, of course,
but there was not. I was dreadfully taken in,
Mr. Pierson.'

Mr. Pierson thought she was not the only
person taken in, but he refrained from saying
so.

'Then,' he went on, 'if anything were to
happen to Mr. Hicks—supposing he died, in
a word—is that six hundred a year so settled
that you would continue to enjoy it as a
widow ?'

' Certainly I should—I suppose——'

' You ought to be *sure*, Lady Hilda,' said Mr. Pierson impressively.

' Why, the man couldn't let me starve.'

' Men have left their widows to starve ; but you can't be serious, Lady Hilda. If the whole of your future had really been in Mr. Hicks's power to make or mar, you would never have so mercilessly ridiculed him and his friends and relations.'

' I only wish I had the chance of getting what I have said about them all in this last book published.'

' Unless you are very certain as to your position I do not think you are wise, Lady Hilda ; but, I beg your ladyship's pardon, I have no right to interfere in an affair which is certainly no business of mine.'

' It is only I who have to suffer,' she answered, in accents of the deepest sincerity ; and then, like Miss Yarlow, she sat for a moment looking earnestly at the fire.

With at least equal earnestness Mr. Pierson looked at her. ' The spell is working,' he thought.

' Heigho !' said her ladyship, at last rising

and gathering her shawl in graceful folds round her still beautiful figure. 'Heigho! you men are all alike—you think of nothing except yourselves. Well, I have not done much good by coming out this wretched day.'

'It is a wretched day,' agreed Mr. Pierson.

'Tell Mr. Vassett I consider he has treated me shamefully, and that I shall advise every person I know never to have anything to do with him.'

'I am very sorry to hear you say so.'

'I do say so. Some day, perhaps, he will regret having let me slip out of his hands; but that will not do me much good.'

She lingered a little longer, only in order apparently to express the same idea again in different words, but at last she took her departure, and Mr. Pierson rushed upstairs to give Mr. Vassett a full account of the interview —full, that is to say, so far as the novel was concerned.

When Mr. Vassett dined at five o'clock, he invited his reader to partake of that meal with him, and during its progress they talked a good deal about Lady Hilda and her book, and the pity it seemed so good a selling author should be lost to Craven Street.

Mr. Vassett was in the act of asking Mr. Pierson if he would take a little more beef, when Muggins appeared with a note, which he said a special messenger had brought from Lady Hilda Hicks. It was directed to the reader, and ran as follows:

'I want to see you at once. Come without a moment's delay.'

Mr. Pierson did not wait for that second helping of meat.

'Finish your dinner,' remonstrated Mr. Vassett; but Mr. Pierson, with a queer smile, said Lady Hilda was of a great deal more importance than dinner.

'Now,' he went on, 'if I can get that book on your own terms, have I *carte blanche* to deal with her?'

Mr. Vassett did not like to be hurried, but he answered, 'Yes;' only adding, 'don't compromise me.'

'You may be sure I shall not do that,' answered Mr. Pierson, and went off joyously.

Before he parted from her ladyship that

evening he had promised to get Mr. Vassett
to publish what Lady Hilda called 'a mutilated
edition' of her novel, to effect a reconciliation
with Mr. Hicks, to so arrange matters that
Royalty should be entertained by her ladyship instead of Miss Hicks, and to endeavour
to procure a sum of money to rid the fair
authoress of some pressing duns.

They separated on the best of terms.

'By-the-bye,' said her ladyship, after bidding
Mr. Pierson 'good-night,' detaining him for a
moment, 'what has become of that girl I saw
at Craven Street one day?'

'I have not seen her for some time,' he
answered.

'She has not set the Thames on fire, then?'

'Not yet,' amended Mr. Pierson; 'not yet.'

CHAPTER V.

MR. LACERE.

'MR. LACERE.'
That was all. Glen bowed, and they became acquainted.

A minute previously and she had been unaware such a person existed; and now, quietly, and as a mere matter of course, he walked into her life to fashion and change the whole of it.

Looking at the stranger by the leaping firelight, she saw a tall, grave man, clad in deep mourning, who to her young eyes seemed quite elderly, and who, in fact, was nearly double her own age.

Certainly not the ideal of male beauty, as that beauty appears to a miss in her teens;

certainly not the hero of Glen's imagination, if an imagination constantly engaged in casting about for heroes of all sorts and aspects and degrees could be supposed to hold one especial image in its innermost recesses.

Like no man, however, she had ever seen before—and at that time Glen considered her experience almost exhaustive, for since the wide field of London was opened to view she had kept an attentive watch both on her own sex and the other, with the view of completely furnishing a gallery of types of character for future use or reference.

A pair of brown eyes glanced down on her with a kindly yet quizzical expression—an expression she learned later on indicated the tenderest heart that ever throbbed, joined to a sense of humour as subtle as it was quiet. Glen was deadly tired, but she did not appear to be so then. On the contrary, coming into the warm room out of the cold evening air, and meeting a visitor when she did not expect to find anyone except her father—the ready blood had rushed to her face—and at the moment she might have stood for a picture of girlish health and strength.

Such beauty as God had given her—and it was not much—happened at the moment to be well in evidence, but Mr. Lacere's calm and inscrutable countenance expressed no admiration as he looked at Mr. Westley's daughter. She did not know then, and she never knew afterwards, what his first impression of her was. Perhaps he could not have told himself, save that he saw the mould she was cast in differed from the pattern of the conventional young women he had hitherto been privileged to meet.

'Glen,' said Mr. Westley, 'Mr. Lacere will have some tea. I had a fall to-day when I was out, and he not merely assisted me to my feet again, but insisted I should sit for a while in his office, and actually accompanied me here. He did not wish to stop, but I told him you would not be long, and——'

'You had a fall, papa?' interrupted Glen a little anxiously, but less anxiously than Mr. Lacere had expected. 'How did it happen?— where did you fall?'

'I do not know how it happened in the least,' answered Mr. Westley. 'I found myself down and I found myself up, thanks to Mr.

Lacere's strong arm and ready help. As to
the where, it was fortunately for me in Sise
Lane, otherwise I might not have met with so
good an example of a modern Samaritan.'

' I am very glad to have been of the slightest
use,' said Mr. Lacere. He had not spoken
since Glen came into the room, and involuntarily she glanced at him once again.

A pleasant voice, but not the voice belonging to that of any hero in Glen's mental
collection. A slight lisp, which, arising more
from shyness than any natural impediment,
disappeared as he grew mo:e at home with his
company; a smile not exactly sad, yet that had
a look akin to sadness underlying it; something about the face, something in the tone,
something in the expression, an indefinable
something pervading the whole man which
arrested Glen's attention and puzzled her !

But she had no prevision that the time
would ever come, when even in memory's
glass she should be unable to see that face
because of a mist of blinding tears ; that the
days were to dawn when, in the morning and
at noon and at evening, she could not speak
aloud his name ; when to hear that voice once

more it would have seemed little to relinquish
fame which had grown valueless, life which
had lost its savour : no, she had no thought or
knowledge or fear of the trouble she was going
on to meet, and yet already she was standing
in the shadows cast by that so far-distant
future, then apparently as remote as the great
dim awful eternity itself.

Meanwhile Mr. Lacere was surprised she
did not evince more concern about her father's
fall. All his life he had lived amongst people
who attached a considerable amount of importance to slight accidents and small ailments,
who were extremely fond of the pastime which
is well known as making mountains out of
molehills, who bemoaned themselves over cut
fingers and burnt hands, and treasured such
accidents as things of great interest and value
in the family archives, and he could not consequently understand an affection which was
not fussy, and fidgety, and foolish. Any one
of these three words he would have repudiated
as utterly inapplicable to the tender feminine
solicitude he had been accustomed to witness ;
but no other could express the useless and
maudlin sympathy some persons are fond of

showing on occasions of no importance, while
they regard with non-comprehending wonder
the wreck of a life—ruined hopes—a broken
heart.

As for Glen, truth to tell, she did not attach
much importance to the accident. When once
her father said nothing was broken or dislocated
or sprained, and that he felt no ill-effects from
his fall, she dismissed the matter from her
mind. In her own London experience—short
though that experience might be considered by
some—she had herself made personal trial of
the hardness of the pavements too often to
regard a tumble—many tumbles, indeed—as
anything abnormal.

So far she had found the thoroughfares so
slippery that to keep up—not to go down—
seemed to her by far the most extraordinary
achievement.

She was now getting a little accustomed to
the ' greasy ' stones and the coal-gratings, and
the slippery basement lights ; and the boys'
slides and the orange peel, and the many other
traps which make London to a new-comer a
terror and a snare ; but in her early days of
metropolitan peregrination she had over and

over again measured her length on the side-
paths, and come down on her knees igno-
miniously, and been greatly indebted for help
to chance passers-by, and become an object of
derision to the street Arabs, and been laughed
at, and been forced to laugh at herself, till it
had become an actual impossibility for her to
conceive of anyone walking day after day and
not at least occasionally ' coming to grief.'

'Let us have tea, dear, soon, will you?'
said Mr. Westley, who, being by this time
pretty well accustomed to the usual lodging-
house delay in the apparently simple matter of
boiling a kettle, felt it necessary to remind
Glen they were not now at Ballyshane, where
no one need ever have waited two minutes for
hot water, where fires had no unhappy way
of ' getting black,' and servants were not in
the habit of turning sulky.

' Yes, papa, I will take off my bonnet at
once;' and Glen turned and left the room and
ran upstairs, just pausing in the passage to ask
the small maid-of-all-work, who always looked
as if she had been blackleading her face instead
of the grate, if she could bring up the
kettle.

' Yes, miss ; I'll make it boil,' was the encouraging answer, an answer the exact meaning
of which Glen knew so well, that meeting the
landlady's daughter, who had just been be-
dizening herself, on the first landing, she said
persuasively :

' Papa wants his tea so much, Miss Dingwell.
Do you think we could have it soon ?'

' Law, yes !' replied Miss Dingwell, who
' bore no malice ' to Glen, though that young
person had refused many well-meant offers to
' take her about a bit.' 'I'll help to get it
ready myself; and you'll like some sort of cake,
won't you ? and if I was you I'd send for a jar
of marmalade and potted beef. Nothing but
bread-and-butter does look so mean ; and
now your beau has come we must make as
much as we can of him.'

Glen turned almost rigid with indignation.

' What are you talking about, Miss Dingwell ?' she exclaimed. ' I never saw the
gentleman before in my life ; and if he does
not like to eat bread-and-butter he must do
without food, for I shall get nothing else for
him '—after which ultimatum, and giving Miss
Dingwell's too-ready tongue no time for retort,

Glen entered her own room and banged the door.

'Well, I'm sure!' exclaimed Miss Dingwell, surveying her own person over her left shoulder with considerable approval; 'I dare say she won't change her dress, or smooth her hair, or anything;' in which surmise Miss Dingwell proved to be both right and wrong.

Glen did smooth her hair, but she did not change her dress. Her heart was very hot within her, for she did not find it easy to forgive or forget such a speech as that made by the fascinating young person who to the country girl's mind seemed the embodiment of everything most hateful and offensive in woman. She had heard of Miss Dingwell's lovers *ad nauseam* — in that house she had grown weary of the word 'man.' It was one of the trials of her then life that their landlady's daughter would persist in thinking she was even such a one as herself. Hitherto Glen had been happily exempt from experiences of this sort. But for this fact her mind might not have been left so free for the 'great work' with which it was occupied; still, just then, even as regarded her mighty enterprise of getting her writings placed before the British public, Glen felt singularly disheartened, and perhaps for this reason Miss Dingwell's blow struck home with double force. At that moment she felt as if doomed to those lodgings for life, as though she would never again be able to get a kettle boiled when she wanted it, or take herself and her belongings beyond reach of people who could scarcely speak, even with the best intentions, without rubbing her sensitive fur the wrong way.

If Miss Dingwell had simpered complaisantly at her own reflection in the glass, not so Glenarva Westley. Fagged and worn, and pale and haggard was the face presented for her consideration by a most unflattering mirror, and she went down into the parlour feeling as satisfied as Mr. Kelly had done 'she was not much to look at.'

Mr. Lacere and her father seemed getting on exceedingly well together, and as the tea-tray, on which Miss Dingwell had considerately placed the second best 'set,' generously adding 'ma's electro pot,' very shortly made its appearance, and the brass kettle followed in its wake with marvellous and unprecedented speed, the awkward pause which ensued upon Glen's appearance proved of short duration.

Mr. Lacere ate bread-and-butter as if he liked it, and the three, who were soon talking, might have known each other for years, so frank and unembarrassed was their conversation.

Just at first Glen felt the unwonted splendour of Mrs. Dingwell's second-best set and the glitter of that electro-plated teapot weigh down her soul ; but she soon took comfort from the reflection that Mr. Lacere could not possibly be acquainted with the pattern of the delft deemed good enough for the everyday use of Mrs. Dingwell's 'parlours,' while his intimacy with the battered Britannia-metal pot was of a similarly negative description ; and her mind being set at rest on these points, she was able to lend an attentive ear to what her father and his visitor were saying—nay, even after a time to join in the talk herself.

'Mr. Lacere tells me, Glen,' observed Mr. Westley, after he had asked his daughter for another cup of tea, ' that we are unwise to remain here—that it is not at all a healthy neighbourhood.'

'Quite the contrary,' said Mr. Lacere.

'Why, I thought,' exclaimed Glen simply, 'that all parts of London were alike. I don't mean as regards fashion, of course,' she went on, as both gentlemen laughed a little at the innocence of her remark.

'Where you are living now,' explained Mr. Lacere, 'was once all a swamp, or rather a lake. You might as well be at the bottom of a well.'

'Oh!' said Glen, not exactly understanding all the pains and penalties attaching to such a position. At Ballyshane people had never thought about healthy or unhealthy localities. Their greatest anxiety was to keep themselves from being blown away by the wild gales which swept down upon them from the Atlantic. A house in a hollow was considered a residence to be desired; and those few trees, which Londoners seem never happy save when they are lopping or grubbing up, were esteemed, in a neighbourhood where it was difficult to get anything except grass as hard as wire to grow, possessions as precious as springs in the desert.

Not all the refuse fish left on the beach to rot, not all the dirt and squalor of some of the poor homes, was able to breed a pestilence. The kindly sea flowed over the sands, and deodorized them twice a day ; and the keen salt breezes carried the poisonous smells far inland from the wretched huts down by the Shane, which were the despair of Mr. Beattie, and a matter of shame to many a sturdy fisherman and his cleanly decent wife.

At that time of the world's history, on the iron-bound, wave-beaten, tempest-tossed coast, so far remote from England and 'civilization,' sanitary arrangements did not possess much interest for a thin, widely scattered population, who had enough to do to earn their daily bread without troubling themselves concerning devices that might add a few years to the length of lives passed in looking death straight in the face—in wresting food for wives and children, indeed, out of its very jaws. No latter-day Solomon had then propounded the theory that by a judicious attention to natural laws people might be enabled to live almost for ever, and for this and other reasons it had not occurred either to Mr. Westley or his daughter that the lodgings they had found were not quite as good as any lodgings they

were likely to find at the price they could afford
to pay for them.

But now Mr. Lacere told them of localities
far pleasanter and no dearer. He seemed to
know London by heart—indeed, he seemed to
understand something about every subject
Mr. Westley touched on.

Looking at their visitor while he was answering a question addressed to him by her father,
Glen wondered vaguely, first, whether he was
in mourning for his wife ; and second, if just
by chance he knew anything concerning the
highways and byways of literature.

A few minutes later she was enlightened,
not indeed concerning his supposed widow-
hood, but as regarded authorship. Mr. Westley, it appeared, had mentioned to him before
she came in that ' his daughter wrote a little
and wished to get into print.' Now Mr.
Lacere reverted to this matter, and said he
was afraid she must find 'going about among
the publishers very discouraging work.'

Glen could have discoursed to some purpose
on this text, but she forebore. She was
getting to feel very doubtful as to whether she
ought ever to have intruded into a publisher's

office. She was losing, she had lost heart altogether. She did not now believe in herself or her fitness to become an author. She had that day been on the pleasing errand of recovering her 'rejected addresses' from the hands of various most unlikely persons, with whom, in her determination to try 'everybody,' it seemed to the girl in her young wisdom well to leave them.

From place to place she trudged valiantly; taking the familiar 'no' with apparently stoical indifference, till at last across one counter a manuscript on which many bright hopes had once been built was handed back to her without a word. Her heart was full, and the trouble may have been evident in her face. At all events she fancied the man *looked* sorry, and that he did not speak because he knew of no word likely to prove of comfort.

Afterwards Glen never could exactly remember how she got out of the office, which was situated on the first floor of a great building in a back lane. She had reached it by means of a wide staircase and a wide landing, and now there was not a creature coming up or going down, and she felt so fairly

'beaten'—no other word in the language fully
expresses the utter weariness which seemed to
oppress both soul and body—that, cowering on
one of the broad easy steps, she covered her
face with her hands, and cried as if her heart
would break, after which exercise she arose
refreshed, and went once more out into the
street to pursue her dreary task.

But Glen said nothing about this experience
then or for many a year afterwards, and in
answer to Mr. Lacere's remark, only replied:

'It does seem very difficult to get a manuscript accepted, but I suppose all authors have
to go through the same ordeal.'

Had Mr. Lacere spoken his mind at that
moment, there can be little doubt he would
have said Miss Westley had better dismiss all
thoughts of authorship from her mind. The
girl did not look as if the making of a writer
was in her—no fire of genius burnt in her
eyes—her expression was not that of a person
so full of imagination that Nature had deemed
well to set her lot apart from the realities of
life. In no solitary respect did Glenarva
Westley fulfil any of the traditional ideas
people have agreed to accept as typifying the

possession of talent—manner, voice, appearance seemed more fitted to the quiet arena of home existence than the mad fight and the fierce Struggle for Fame. It was hard upon Glenarva that no human being ever believed she was the right person in the right place. Not when she was plodding amongst the London publishers—not when she was making a little money—not when she had gained a great reputation—not when the time came no one could deny she had achieved more than nine hundred and ninety-nine women out of a thousand ever do achieve—no, not even then did any friend, or relation, or stranger realize it was really Glenarva who had won success, and not some quite independent power associated with her in an unaccountable and uncanny sort of alliance.

Mr. Kelly had thought nothing of her personal appearance. Mr. Lacere, certainly, did not regard Glenarva as a shrine in which it seemed particularly probable genius had chosen to take up an abode. He saw before him a slight, young, underfed-looking girl, who appeared to him deficient in physique, and still more deficient in will. No two more incompetent individuals, he conceived, had ever come to London on a wild-goose chase than Miss Westley and her father. Had he heard the words uttered by the steward of the Morecambe steamer, 'God help them; they are no better nor a couple of children,' he would have echoed them cordially.

But he felt heartily sorry for the poor gentleman and his daughter. He knew what a lonely wilderness London must seem to them, and he did not believe it would be a true kindness to disillusion the girl at once.

She would find in time she had no true mission to become a writer; he would not cross her whim, he would not say what he thought about the absurdity of her writing. He would do what he could to help her.

' Yes,' he said, ' all young authors find publishers a little impracticable at first, but it is a mere question of time. Sooner or later genius must obtain a hearing.'

' Ah ! but it is such a long time,' exclaimed Glen, with involuntary sadness, ' and it is generally so much later than sooner.'

' Why,' exclaimed Mr. Lacere, ' you are surely not beginning to despair yet ! You have not, I think, been in London six months!'

'No,' said Mr. Westley, answering for his daughter, who did not seem inclined to do so for herself; 'we only left Ireland in October, and of course, as you observe, she has all her life before her in which to make her mark.'

Mr. Lacere had not adventured on any observation of the sort, but, understanding perfectly that ¡ Glenarva's father was merely putting into his visitor's mouth the idea with which he sought to comfort and reassure himself, he allowed the utterance to pass unnoticed, and said to the girl, kindly :

'Very probably that time seems like six years to you.'

'It seems a long time,' agreed Glenarva, but she added no other syllable of explanation; she did not speak of the events, persons, disappointments, bodily weariness, actual physical hardships, which had caused the period of their residence in London to lengthen itself out so unduly.

Looks, however, occasionally can talk more eloquently than tongues; and Mr. Lacere gathered from the expression of Glenarva's

face at that moment some knowledge of what
the girl never could have spoken in words.

It then occurred to him to ask her if she
had seen all the sights, and which of them impressed her most.

'I have not seen any of them,' she answered,
'except Westminster Abbey and St. Paul's.
We generally go to service at the Abbey on
Sunday afternoons.'

'But do you not think it would prove an
agreeable change if you were to visit a few, at
all events, of the places strangers generally go
to see?'

Glen did not seem to know. She said sight-
seeing would take up a great deal of time, and,
she might have added, money also, only she
was not likely to bring that question on the
tapis.

'Have you been to any of the theatres?'
persisted Mr. Lacere, talking to these people
as he would have talked to those amongst
whom his previous lot had chanced to be cast.

'No,' answered the girl; 'papa does not care
for places of amusement, and neither do I.'

And Glen looked as if she and her father
were persons who, having run the whole

round of innocent dissipation and exhausted its pleasures, had resolved to settle down for ever to a quiet, humdrum, Darby and Joan sort of life.

In spite of himself, Mr. Lacere smiled. He could not help it.

'And so,' he went on, 'since your arrival in London you have done nothing except try to make an impression upon the publishers, who are so stony-hearted and so difficult to impress?'

'I think I have been to them all,' answered Glenarva, 'and it has taken me a long time, because,' she added apologetically, 'places are so far apart in London.'

'They are, but you find the omnibuses very convenient.'

'I scarcely ever go in one,' said the girl. 'I always walk.'

'Always walk! Why, you must get very tired.'

'I should not get tired if the streets were not so slippery,' she replied.

'My daughter is a capital walker,' explained Mr. Westley.

'Yes. We hadn't many omnibuses at

Ballyshane,' Glen said, with a touch of merriment Mr. Lacere had not heard in her voice previously; and then she went on to tell him about Ballyshane—about its cliffs and its bogs, and its magnificent views, and its loneliness, and the wild tempests that washed the salt spray so far inland, and the waves rippling in on' the shore when the weather was fine and calm, and the crested billows that came thundering in from the Atlantic in the stormy winter-time, billows pursued by other billows that raced over the sunken rocks, and beat themselves madly to death against the great headlands that frowned above the ocean ; and Mr. Lacere said he should like to see that grand desolate coast, and Glenarva thought she would too—but she did not say so. She sat silent while Mr. Westley, taking up her parable, spoke of the geological formation of that part of Ireland, and told Mr. Lacere many things concerning the Giants' Causeway, Fairhead, and Carrick-a-rede, and the Cushendall Caves, and the Salmon Leaps at Coleraine, which were strange to that gentleman, and impressed him with the same sense of unreality as a fairy-tale might have done.

And all the time Glenarva was recalling sadly the dream she had dreamed—looking out over the sea, and wandering across the cliffs, and traversing the road leading to Artinglass, and writing in her bedroom, with the roses peeping in at the window to see what she was doing, or tapping against the glass to win her out into the sunshine flooding the whole landscape with a glamour of golden light.

Then suddenly the past faded away utterly, and she was back in dreary, shabby London lodgings : all her hopes as dead as last year's roses, the sunshine gone, stern reality around instead of a golden glamour, and Mr. Lacere looking at her intently.

'I think,' he said gently, reverting to the one subject which at that time was of paramount interest to Glenarva, 'you are expending your strength uselessly in going about among all the publishers. A vast number of them can never be of the slightest benefit to you. Why not confine yourself to a few good houses ?'

'What is the use,' asked the girl, 'when they will not read what I take them ?'

'Why not try to write something they will read?'

'I do not exactly understand what you mean,' said Glen.

'What I mean is this,' answered her new friend, 'that writing, like everything else in the world, requires pains and practice. I see you have been at work at some pretty embroidery——' he suddenly added, with all a man's deep appreciation of that purely feminine art.

'Glen is very fond of work,' said Glen's father; and, indeed, this statement was true in its widest sense.

At that time, whatever her hands found to do the girl did with all her might. Idleness seemed to her then an impossible condition of existence. She would rather have hemmed dusters for Mrs. Dingwell than done nothing; and as she found the small amount of mending required by her own and her father's wardrobe insufficient to occupy her leisure-time, now she found writing so difficult as to be impossible, she had bought some designs stamped in blue outlines on white muslin, and was embroidering herself a pair of cuffs and a collar.

'Well, go back to the time when you first began to learn to sew,' said Mr. Lacere, with that look in his eyes that had already become familiar to Glen. 'You could not have filled in all this delicate tracery of leaf, and stem, and flower then;' and he took the fragile scrap of work in his hand almost tenderly as he spoke, and looked at it as he was never likely to look at any manuscript with which she might present him.

'No, indeed,' said Glen, laughing in spite of herself. 'I remember quite well my first essay in that line. It was made with a pin, to which my nurse securely tied a piece of strong thread; and I had for material a strip of flannel, and each time I dragged the pin through the flannel I made a hole as large as that,' and she touched one in the collar — called, as Mr. Lacere heard from her subsequently, a 'wheel.'

'Yet now see what you can do,' he remarked, looking at the elaborate pattern worked in by Glen's fine needle. 'And as regards your writing,' he went on, 'it may be that some day hereafter you will think of your present efforts as you do of the strip of flannel disfigured with holes. I have known many beginners, and the mistake they seem to make is that they imagine writing comes by inspiration. Of course, unless a person has a certain aptitude—or genius, if you prefer the word—no amount of time and patience can enable him to produce a book worth reading; but I do not believe any genius, however great it may be, will ever carry a man to success without the help of dogged perseverance and determined plodding on his own part.'

'But I have plodded, and have persevered,' pleaded Glen, with almost tearful earnestness.

'For how long? for a few weeks?' suggested Mr. Lacere.

'No; for years, and years, and years.'

'You must have begun, then, before you could walk, I should think.'

'She did begin very early,' interposed Mr. Westley; 'and I do not see at all, Glen, why you should feel so dissatisfied with your success. I am sure since you came to London you have had a vast amount of encouragement.'

'In words, papa.'

'What do the publishers say to you, Miss Westley?' inquired Mr. Lacere, determined to obtain some explicit answer.

' Well, a few of them say I can write,' answered Glenarva, maintaining a wise silence concerning the many who said nothing at all ;. ' but no one I have met with as yet will really read a manuscript. I have only written Irish stories, and they want English.'

' Then why do you not write English stories for them ?' naturally inquired Mr. Lacere.

Glen did not reply, so her father said :

' I fancy she has nôt felt much inclined for writing lately.'

' No ?' interrogated Mr. Lacere, with a sympathetic expression of countenance, but in reality pleased to hear this. There never yet lived a wise man who wished women to turn artists, or actresses, or authors ; and Mr. Lacere, theoretically at least, was a wise man. By some subtle intuition he knew Glen would be far happier if she never gained a hearing—if she laid aside her manuscripts as a child lays aside its toys which have pleased it for a while, and betook herself to the business of life, as such business usually presents itself to her sex —taking her pleasure while she could, mixing with other young people, going to places of amusement ; then being loved and loving ;

then marrying and ruling her husband's household.

Mentally he went through all this catalogue of recreations and duties while Mr. Westley was saying :

' She has not been quite well lately. I am beginning to think, with you, this neighbourhood does not suit either of us.'

' It is most depressing,' observed Mr. Lacere. ' I am sure you ought not to remain in it ;' and he made this remark with such thorough conviction, that when shortly afterwards he rose to go Mr. Westley said :

' We will take your advice and look out for other lodgings at once.'

' But you will let me know where you decide to settle,' answered Mr. Lacere quickly. ' I may be able to prove of some assistance to your daughter.'

' I shall certainly keep you informed of our address, since you are so good as to wish to have it ;' and then the three shook hands cordially, and quite like old acquaintances, and when the door closed behind their visitor Mr. Westley said :

' What a kind man, Glen ! I really shall

begin to consider that a most fortunate fall of mine which brought me into contact with him;' but Glenarva did not answer. She was thinking at that moment of Mr. Lacere less as a pleasant acquaintance than as a person who might be able to help forward her great work.

'We will at once, dear, begin looking out for different lodgings,' went on Mr. Westley, not noticing his daughter's silence.

She woke up as though out of a dream.

'If you remember, papa, I told you a little time ago there were some rooms advertised near Russell Square I thought seemed cheap; but you fancied nothing we could live in was likely to be had in that neighbourhood at a moderate price.'

'But I find London has changed since I knew anything about it,' he answered. 'What a pity we did not inquire concerning them at the time.'

'I kept the address,' she said.

'Then, Glen, you had better go and see what the rooms are like to-morrow.'

'Very well, papa,' she answered, more than willing to take all the trouble she could off his hands, and quite unconscious of what her

father's growing disposition to leave such bur-
dens for her to carry really meant. Looking
back afterwards she understood, and thanked
God earnestly her strength had been great and
her spirit willing; that wind or weather, fog,
frost, or snow never kept her within doors
when there existed any need for her to be out;
that it was she who usually faced the stinging
cold of that cruel winter, and who saw to
everything a girl might, and to many things
most girls never do.

Next day she came back radiant, looking as
Mr. Westley had not seen her look since they
left Ballyshane.   The rooms were still vacant,
and they were such pleasant, cosy rooms, but
very high up—two on the second floor and one
on the third.   The people wanted to let them
to persons who would not require much attend-
ance, ' so if we go there,' proceeded Glen, 'we
shall not have another Miss Dingwell dancing
in and out all day long.'   For indeed that
young lady was somewhat apt to introduce her
presence uninvited and unwished-for, and she
had a knack of making a fresh scuttleful of
coals an excuse for a long conversation, and the
removal of the tea-tray an opportunity for

gossip, which wore the thread of Glen's patience almost to its last strand.

After some hesitation Mr. Westley decided to take the rooms of which his daughter spoke so highly, and though the ground was covered with snow and the sky was black and lowering with the promise of more, they very shortly transported themselves and their belongings to that part of London called the Bloomsbury district, where for the first time Glen began really to enjoy her metropolitan experiences, and to think some pleasure might be extracted from life, even in a great town 'where one knew nobody.'

Ere long she commenced writing again with something of the frenzy and fervour of old. She got through an enormous amount of work —such as it was—in the dull, dark days of that most dreary winter. Her spirits revived. She could still imagine and record her imaginings. She had a story which was perfectly true to tell, and she told it on page after page of blotted foolscap. It was a story of sin and sorrow and injustice, or what seemed to her injustice. There had been a time when she would have hesitated to present it in any form to the public, but she had left Ballyshane now far behind her on the road of life ; no one there knew she wrote; she could utilize her experiences without the fear of giving offence.

She brought all her Irish characters over to England, and planted them on a wild portion of the Yorkshire coast.   She knew nothing in the world about the coast she described, but that was a matter of detail which troubled Glen as little in those days as it seems to trouble many authors in these.   Had anyone hinted that her English peasants were not true to Nature, and her lords and ladies creations almost as impossible, she would not have believed the statement ; but no one did hint anything of the sort, for which reason Glen's latest barque glided swiftly over the sea of fiction, leaving a trail of inky paper behind it, and the girl pressed hopefully onward, feeling quite satisfied she was at length producing something the world would not willingly let die.

Poor Glen !   In the whole of London I doubt if there was then a happier girl than she who from that second floor beheld in fancy the golden gates of Fame opening to admit her.

She had secured a publisher—found a man

at last who said if she liked to write him a good novel of English life he would be at the expense of bringing it out ; and he said more also, namely, that he would give her thirty pounds for another if her first book succeeded as he believed it would.

He was a gentleman who seemed to have less to do than any person she had yet come across in London ; but he had published a great many books, and known a great many authors, and over the fire in his inner office the pair held many long and delightful conversations.

He told her the amount he had paid this person and that ; what a *Times* review was worth ; how novel-publishing was going to the dogs ; wondered what the end of it all would prove ; waxed confidential concerning his own domestic affairs ; and one day when Glen, having contrived to cut her hand badly, appeared with it bandaged and in a sling, advised her as to her treatment of the wound with an earnestness he could scarcely have surpassed had her management of an intricate and exciting plot been the theme.

But, notwithstanding the friendly relations thus established between them, the ungrateful

young author decided she would not give him
that wonderful book with which she meant to
astonish the British public.

In the course of her peregrinations amongst
all sorts and conditions of men engaged in the
book trade, she found out that though the individual in question was supposed to have 'made
a lot of money' by 'working the libraries'—
an utterance which seemed Delphic in its obscurity to the girl's then unenlightened mind—
he was not by any means at the 'top of the tree.'

' Pedland is well enough in his way, but he
does not stand like Hurst and Blackett, or
Chapman and Hall, or the other great guns,'
explained one uncommonly common publisher
in the Row, while the next time she saw her
new friend she was privileged to hear from
him what he thought of the ' great guns.'
Had Glen only availed herself fully of the
educational advantages offered to her at that
time concerning the ways of publishers, she
might have been qualified to write an exhaustive treatise on the race ; but the girl was
too much taken up with her own doings to pay
the attention she ought to have done to the
doings of other people.

A confused notion that she was 'getting on' somehow; that by some unintelligible means she was pushing herself to the front, was all she seemed thoroughly to grasp. Mr. Lacere told her she was doing too much, but his words of wisdom fell on heedless ears.

In those days Glen thought nothing of writing a novel. She turned one out in a month for the gentleman who 'worked the libraries.' She herself thought of it as 'quite good enough,' and really it was not so bad.

But, good or bad, Mr. Pedland seemed no more ready to read her manuscript when completed than anybody else. He said he 'had not time; that the season was past; that he would attend to her presently; that she would have to take her turn; that really the number of authors who wrote remarkably well was getting so great he could not imagine how their books were ever to be published; that the libraries were overstocked; that he could get novels with well-known names on the title-page for a song, a mere song; that he could remember the time when he was glad to pay so-and-so a hundred pounds down for any manuscript he liked to bring, and now,' finished

this modern Jeremiah, 'I should think twice
before I gave him a hundred shillings.'

He told her rival houses were ruining the
trade, 'cutting each other's throats;' and then,
having depressed her spirits to zero, he said if
she looked in again in a few weeks' time he
might be able to talk to her.

But Glen was not exactly made of the stuff
to bear this sort of thing with equanimity.

She said she would not look in again in a
few weeks' time, and that if he had not time
to read her manuscript she should like to take
it back with her.

Then he promised to look at it, and failed to
do so. He always found some good reason
for escaping from his duties—his wife had
been ill, or he had been ill himself; or he was
called suddenly out of town; or a man who
owed him a heavy account had gone into the
Gazette, and he was forced to rush off to the
Land's End in order to see if a dividend of a
penny in the pound could be rescued out of
the wreck.

He provoked Glen, and amused her too. In
the after-times she always retained a certain
grateful memory of that snug old publishing

establishment, where the office was so quiet, and the fire so large, and the easy-chairs so comfortable, and where she heard so much, true and false, concerning the inner life of literature, and the dealings of printers, and publishers, and authors, and editors. Spite even of herself she was learning a great deal, and she never returned to those second-floor lodgings without a budget of news ready to be unfolded for her father's benefit.

One afternoon in the early spring, when barrows filled with flowers were just beginning to appear in the streets, when the winter weather seemed gone, and the snow had at last disappeared, and a blue sky stretched over-head, and the sun shone occasionally for half an hour or so at a time, Glen was making her way back from the west when she ran up against Mr. Pierson, who, greeting her with the greatest cordiality, remarked she was quite a stranger in Craven Street.

'You have deserted us totally,' he said. 'Why don't you come and see Mr. Vassett ?'

'Mr. Vassett does not want to see me,' Glen answered, a little saucily.

'Oh ! but he does,' declared Mr. Pierson,

with that utter disregard of truth which was one of his distinguishing qualities. 'We were talking about you only the other day, and wondering what had become of you. Now that the fine weather is here, it is a thousand pities you should not call and have a talk with Vassett. You had better look in as soon as you can ; to-morrow if you like. He is in very good twist now, though I suppose you don't know what I mean by that.'

'Oh yes, I do,' said Glen, who had not grown up on terms of familiar intimacy with six graceless boys for nothing.

'Well, then, step round to-morrow, and tell us what you have been about for so long.'

Glen laughed, and said she would, and as she pursued her onward way felt more and more satisfied she was getting 'well to the front.'

CHAPTER VI.

STRANDED.

T has been previously hinted that when Mr. Westley arrived in England he brought with him across the Channel a project for improving his worldly condition, but with the reticence which was so marked a feature in his character he did not consider it necessary to communicate his idea to Glen.

Of himself he never would have summoned up enough energy to travel to London with it; but as his daughter wished to put her fortunes to the test at the headquarters of literature, and as Mr. Merritt urged him strongly to leave Ireland, and advanced enough money for the purpose, Mr. Westley arrived in Babylon as has been chronicled; and, stimulated perhaps by the rush and movement all around, and by a host of olden memories associated with his pleasant youth, the poor gentleman donned the best suit he had in his possession, and started off one day to Bolton Row, Mayfair, where resided the former friend to whom he had once been mentor and companion, and who had since those days become Marquis of Thanet.

It was not till he stood on the very doorstep that a doubt of how he might be received crossed Mr. Westley's mind, but even this passing cloud soon disappeared from his sky; he had been only after a fashion a dependent then, and he was going to ask for nothing save employment now. He had been rich and considered since he parted with Lord Charles; but all the prosperity, and the greatness, and the ruin wrought by his own folly, and the gradual descent into the valley of poverty, were matters quite independent of the life which had been his when he mixed intimately with lords and ladies, and the door of the house before which he now stood was opened wide for him to enter as a matter of course.

He had a tale to tell, a petition to prefer. He did not much doubt the result. Too many kindnesses had been showered upon him in the past to permit him to fear repulse or coldness now. All he regretted was not having sooner thought of so excellent a plan for improving his prospects. He had mooned away years in idleness and vain regrets when he might have been making money for his child. Well, it was late in the day, certainly, but better late than never; and so with a courage which had in it no trace of assurance, Mr. Westley knocked at the once familiar door.

His knock was answered by a servant out of livery, who said his lordship was not in, and he did not exactly know any hour when he could certainly be found. His lordship was merely in town for a few days, *en route* from Rome to Brushwood, and was very rarely to be found at Bolton Row. No, he did not think he could be met with at his club; but 'if you will leave your name, sir,' he added, with a certain amount of doubt and hesitation Mr. Westley did not at the moment understand, and which vexed him unreasonably in consequence.

31—2

' I will write to his lordship,' he said, taking out his card and giving it to the man, who exclaimed with a certain bewildered wonderment, 'Mr. Westley! it is not, surely—and yet I thought, sir, there was something about you I remembered.'

' Why, are you Harling?' asked Mr. Westley. ' How you are changed! You were but a mere stripling when I saw you last.'

' Yes, sir; won't you walk in? Pray do. His lordship may return presently, though we never know when to expect him. He would be sorry, I am sure, to miss seeing you. Yes, sir, as you observe, it is many years since that day at Nice when the news came for you to go to Ireland.'

Many years indeed! yet as he looked once more round the well-remembered room, they seemed to Mr. Westley but as few and evil as those of his pilgrimage appeared to the patriarch of old.

' The late Marquis often talked about you, sir, and said over and over again if ever he went to Dublin he would try and get up to your place in the north.'

' Which I have lost and left for ever, Harling,' answered Mr. Westley. It was not his nature to trade upon the feelings of his fellows and seek for sympathy in his misfortunes ; but neither could he pose as a man still possessed of fortune before this servant, who knew that when they last parted he left a life of obscurity in order to take up a position amongst those who, by virtue both of birth and wealth, rank amongst the Upper Ten.

'Indeed, sir ; I am very sorry to hear you say so. I do not think the late Marquis knew anything about that, or he would have mentioned it to me ; for he often spoke about you, he did indeed.'

'Harling,' said Mr. Westley, looking at the man with sudden anxiety, 'whom do you mean when you talk about the "late" Marquis ? surely not——'

'Lord Charles ? Yes, indeed, sir ; he died quite suddenly. Is it possible you have not heard ?'

Mr. Westley stopped the speaker with a gesture of grief and dismay. Dead ! Then all his hopes were dead too, and yet at that moment it was not of himself he was thinking ; it was of the frank, generous nobleman stricken

down in his prime, of the face he remembered
flushed with boyish health, and the frame full
of youthful strength now cold and quiet in
death.

'You did not notice the hatchment, then,
sir ?' asked Harling, after a pause.

'No ; I walked on this side of the way.
And the present Marquis is ?'

'His brother—Lord Louis, sir, you remember. The late Marquis left no children. But
you will wait a few minutes longer, Mr. Westley, will you not? I am sure his lordship
would like to see you.'

' No, oh no, thank you. I did not know, or
I should not have intruded. Tell the Marquis
how grieved I am to hear of his loss, and——'

' Here is his lordship,' interrupted Harling,
and he hurried away to inform the new Marquis that Mr. Westley was in the library,
while Mr. Westley himself stood in the middle
of the room irresolute, not liking to go into
the hall for fear of encountering a person who
perhaps might not wish to see him, and liking
almost less to remain, lest it should seem as
though he did not mean to leave without com-
pelling an interview.

But his doubts were next moment laid at rest by the Marquis himself, who, dressed in the deepest mourning, entered the apartment, and, addressing him most cordially, said how heartily sorry he was his brother was not alive to greet his old friend.

They had always loved each other tenderly, those two sons of the old Marquis, and it seemed a comfort to the one that was left to talk about the dead man to a person who had formerly been in daily and familiar companionship with him.

'Will you come and dine here quietly?' asked the Marquis. 'I am only in town on my way to Brushwood, and everything is in confusion—it was so sudden, so unexpected, poor fellow; but still, if you can spare an hour or two——'

Mr. Westley hastened to excuse himself as the other paused, and then in a few sentences he told why he had come, and what he had wanted to ask.

'Perhaps,' he added hesitatingly, 'you might hear of something, and——'

'You may feel quite sure I shall do all that lies in my power to forward your wishes,' said the Marquis. 'Leave me your address, and should any idea occur to my mind before I see you again I will write at once. Come to dinner, though. We shall be quite alone. No? Well, then, if it must be so, good-bye for the present. I shall think over what you have told me, and consider the best way to serve your interests.'

Time is one quantity to those who wait, and quite another to those who are not waiting. The days and the weeks and the months which slipped by after Mr. Westley's visit to Bolton Row may not have seemed long in passing to the new Marquis, who had just succeeded to a great property, who had to see lawyers and stewards and friends and relations, and whose time was occupied from morning till night by the claims of Society and the thousand details to which he was forced to give his attention ; but to the ruined gentleman in narrow lodgings, with most limited means, with poor health, without society or occupation, or anything pleasant to reflect upon in the present or to look forward to in the future—how did that period appear?

Ah ! not Glen herself waiting for the ' No '

she said certainly must come, but which for all that she did not expect, experienced a greater trouble and sickness at her heart than her father, who kept his disappointment to himself, and felt he was forgotten by fortune and forsaken by man.

It was the last straw his feeble hand strove to clutch. He knew he could do nothing more. He could not write and remind Lord Thanet of his promise ; it was impossible for him to go and knock again at the once familiar door, and ask if the Marquis had heard of anything to suit him.

There are persons who can lie down and die and utter no complaint, or, sitting alone beside a fireless hearth, will starve and make no sign. Mr. Westley was one of these. For his daughter's sake he, a shipwrecked castaway on the world's wide ocean, hoisted that one. feeble signal of distress ; but he could not continue holding out the flag. As help failed to come to him he let this last hope drop from his nerveless fingers, and resigned himself to the conviction that if anything were to be done for Glen, it must be done by Glen herself.

The girl could not imagine why her father was so anxious she should punctually fulfil the promise she had made Mr. Pierson.

Somehow she was not very desirous of keeping her appointment in Craven Street, and said that after all she did not think it was worth while wasting the time it would take to walk there.

'I am quite certain Mr. Vassett will not look at any one of my manuscripts,' she declared; but Mr. Westley told her she could not tell what the publisher might do unless she asked him.

'I thought him most kind and courteous,' said Mr. Westley; hearing which, Glen laughingly suggested he should go in her place.

'You can go and talk to him, papa,' she observed; but her father did not see the beauty of this proposition.

He had never been able to understand how Glen could walk into shops and offices and ask to see editors and publishers. He supposed, as she did not seem to suffer either anguish or shame, there was nothing wrong in her going about as she did; but he felt she must possess or lack some quality which in his own nature

was either non-existent or else developed to an
undue excess.

Poor Mr. Westley ! He had never attempted
to analyze any character ; not even his own.
And yet sometimes, as he noted his daughter's
tireless energy and her dogged industry, the
idea occurred to him that, regarded as a soldier
in the battle of life, he was but a poor feeble
creature, and that the sensitiveness which made
him shrink from the noise and the bustle, the
clang of tongues and the call to arms, was less
a virtue than a vice.

What had his pride—which after all was not
an unworthy or an ignoble or a sinful pride—
done for him ? Now he was beginning dimly
to comprehend that even when the worst came
—when he lost money and lands and home—
he might to a certain extent have retrieved
his error had he, instead of avoiding his fellows
and sinking into a melancholy recluse, turned
a brave face to the world, tried if there was
not something still left his hand could find to
do, and determined, in the face of blackest
fortune, to ' quit himself like a man.'

He could not understand his daughter, but
dimly he was coming to the comprehension

that what she found possible he ought to have found possible also.

There is nothing much more sad or pitiful than this awakening in age to the knowledge of a defect possible only for youth to remedy. When the blood is growing cold and the pulse slow, and the limbs feeble, and the heart weary, how shall we take up a burden we thought too heavy to carry in the noontide of our strength, and bear it triumphantly home ? At the eleventh hour it is possible for a man to repent, but it is as a rule impossible for him to repair the evil he has wrought.

The day of work is behind him—the night of death, when no man can work, before; and what shall he who has permitted all the long hours of light to glide away unimproved do in those brief minutes when the evening gloom is darkening down apace, and the long shadows cast from that land which to us is all mystery, are lying athwart the path his laggard feet must tread ? O God ! if it might only be as some modern divines tell us, that in the world where we are lonely journeying ' we may undo much that we have done here wrongly ; do again with perfect grace that which we have done imperfectly ; become what we have aimed and wished to be ; achieve what we have longed to achieve ; attain the wisdom, the gifts, and powers to which we have aspired ;' who is there that would not long to leave the old and begin the new, and to enter on that life which, as Dickens, apparently inspired by the same idea, says, ' sets this one right'!

As is not unusual in cases where men have left their own noontide hours unimproved, Mr. Westley grew day by day more anxious that his daughter, on whom the hopeful glory of morning still shone in all its brightness, should make the most of her opportunities.

He did not talk to her of fame. Indeed, the idea of Glen, his Glen, ever making for herself a name and a position seemed to him inconceivable. As we know, ' a man is not without honour save in his own country and amongst his own people,' and there are very good reasons for this. It is hard to realize that which has been with us in common achieving something uncommon ; the child we have taught to walk, climbing to heights our feet cannot scale ; the girl we have hushed to rest wandering out of the sweet home life to be greeted by the

world's applause! After all, it is only what
we see we really believe, and therefore when
before our eyes the boy stands on the dizzy
height and the girl smiles back to us through
happy tears, with the laurel crown resting on
the sunny tresses of yore, we come dimly to
understand there was something in them we
wot not of. We cannot begin our day with a
forecast of its end; and if we were wise—
which we are not, any one of us—we should
be able to comprehend that, though we may
bend over a child in its cradle, it is not given
to us to know the bed in which it will lie when
life's long dream is over. It may be Westminster Abbey, a felon's grave, a hundred
fathoms of water, or the shallow hole hurriedly
dug on the field of battle where he gave up
his life for duty and his country!

So to come back. Though Mr. Westley
hoped and believed Glen would make a few
pounds a year by her pen—which implement
he spoke of as he might her needle—he never
really thought, save for a few wild moments,
his daughter had it in her to do great things.

He saw her writing, about which she set in
a prosaic, domestic sort of way that perplexed

him exceedingly. If Mr. Westley wished to
write an important letter, the decks had to be
cleared for the purpose. It was while Glen
was out of the way he indited those epistles to
his lawyer which that gentleman regarded, and
not without reason, as the embodiments of so
much time and labour lost. If, on the contrary, Glen decided to commence a quite new
novel, which perhaps she did after five minutes'
consideration, she put on her bonnet, went out
and bought a few quires of foolscap, set to
work stitching the pages together into dozens,
and began.

Yes, then and there, with an old pen, the
top of which she had bitten almost through
when struggling with the intricacies of an
involved sentence, or the difficulties of a far-
fetched comparison. Writing seemed no
trouble to her at that period, and an outsider might well be excused the argument
that what cost so little could not be worth
much.

Ah! the day of her travail was then afar off
—the hour when, in sorrow and in agony, she
produced a living, breathing book ; something
with the imprint of God upon it, a coin

stamped with the superscription of that mint which sends nothing into circulation except the gold of genius.

Nevertheless, Mr. Westley believed she would get on ; perhaps he was afraid to think of the depths of poverty she might have to sound otherwise—but that is beside the question.

'Take that last tale of yours, dear, down with you to Mr. Vassett,' he said. 'Who knows what may happen ?'

'I know, papa,' she answered. 'He will not look at it.'

'Still, I would take it, dear. You believe yourself it is very good, don't you ?'

'What do you believe, papa ?' she asked, with a smile which told her own opinion of the work.

'Well, Glen, I can't say I profess to be a judge, yet I think it ought to be liked. To tell the truth, however, it seems to me you never have surpassed, and you never will surpass, that chapter you wrote at Ballyshane the evening you had been out on the cliffs.'

'But that is so dreadfully Irish !' objected Glen, quoting some of her critics.

And, in good earnest, this was a difficulty the girl happened then to be contending against. She did not know enough of England to write about it—no, not even the aspect of nature in England. How could one accustomed to that wild sea, to those tossing billows, to the lonely rocks where the seagulls built, the stretching moorlands, the desolate bogs, and the sullen headlands frowning darkly on the Atlantic—write of gliding streams and flower-decked meadows, of the great, open, red-tiled barns she had not yet seen, or strawyards, or cowslips, or any one of the thousand sights which render an English landscape so pre-eminently dear to all who love the English word Home?

She knew nothing about the homestead as it appears to the eyes of the youngest English child; she was still an alien, though learning to love and admire the country of her adoption. She regarded everything as an Englishman might the sights and sounds and customs of a foreign city. So far, the land and the people and the customs of the nation lay outside her; and it was not till they became soul of her soul, and heart of her heart, Glen moved the souls and hearts of those she wrote for. Till there were tears in the music she made, till she sobbed out the words of her lay, and felt the warmth herself of the sunshine she bade others bask in, success did not come to Glenarva Westley, spite of the fact that she followed her father's advice, and took with her to Craven Street the Benjamin of her life, the ' last, best, sweetest, strongest book,' according to her own estimate, she had as yet written to astonish an ungrateful world.

When she arrived at the publisher's, Muggins, who seemed plunged into a depth of gloom which nothing save impending bankruptcy on the part of his employer and an execution in his own home could possibly have justified, informed her Mr. Vassett was out, and Mr. Pierson engaged three deep.

' You can wait if you like, you know,' he said ; but something in his tone induced Glen, whose temper was rather of the hottest, to say she should like to do nothing of the kind, and she was turning to leave the outer office when Mr. Vassett himself entered.

' Oh ! and how do you do ?' he exclaimed, not seeming, however, in the least degree glad to

see her, which fact Glen felt acutely as she
answered :

'I am very well, thank you. No, I did not
want anything—only I told Mr. Pierson I
should call to-day.'

'As you are here, come in,' suggested Mr.
Vassett. 'Eh, what did you say?'—this to
Muggins, who was making various telegraphic
signs to his employer.

'Lady Hilda's there, and Mr. Pierson, and
the actor gentleman, and some one he has
brought with him.'

'Well, just come in then, will you?' said
Mr. Vassett, with a certain irritation in his
tone Glen did not fail to notice.

By this time she knew all about Lady
Hilda. Mr. Pedland had given her the full
story of the Hicks alliance, had told the girl
every scandal there was to tell on the subject
—true and false. Miss Westley's six months'
term of study in the Metropolitan Academy
had taught her many things about authors and
authoresses Mr. Vassett did not know. Flitting
about from place to place, she heard every
piece of gossip worth hearing ; she was a good
listener, and often and often when pacing the

back streets homewards—for Glen's knowledge of London within a certain radius was even then almost exhaustive—she laughed softly to herself over the stories she was carrying back to that cheap second floor in Bloomsbury, while the passers-by turned with a quick, sympathetic look in their faces, wondering who the girl could be, and what she was smiling at with such thorough, though quiet, enjoyment while she passed swiftly along.

Lady Hilda was more radiant than ever. She was in the highest spirits, and greeted Mr. Vassett with effusion. She playfully called him a 'grumpy old dear,' and said, after the success of her book, she expected to see his face bright with smiles instead of gloomy as a November day.

'If you take my advice,' she said to Glen, 'you won't have anything to do with him. I never mean him to publish another book of mine.'

'One side of a story is good till another is told,' remarked Mr. Pierson.

'Now, don't *you* begin to be disagreeable,' exclaimed the lady. 'Mr. Vassett, I wish you had stayed away. We were all as comfortable

and pleasant as possible till you came in.
You might serve for the skeleton at a
feast—and that reminds me I want you to
come to *my* feast. The great day is at
hand. Blow the trumpets, sound the drums!
the noble building for Decayed Fishwives
is to be opened on the 20th by one of
the Blood Royal, whom we are afterwards
to have the honour to receive at luncheon,
and all the county people are expected in
force, and everybody in the City who has a
million of money and upwards ; and I shall
not be happy unless you witness my triumph.
You won't refuse. Now do—*do*—DO say I
may count on seeing you !'

But Mr. Vassett utterly refused to say anything of the kind. She could not cajole or
scold him into compliance, so at last, saying
' he was a horrid creature,' she turned in
despair to Mr. Pierson, and entreated that he
at least would not desert her.

For a time she went on in this way, dealing
out invitations like a pack of cards, and receiving for answer only murmured apologies
or amused smiles, till it occurred to her the
' bread-and-butter ' girl, who was sitting a little

in the background, had not been included in the game.

'You can come too, if you like,' she said, nodding to her over the barricade formed by Mr. Dawton's right shoulder.

Glen was not stricken dumb with indignation at this cavalier address, because she answered it, but her voice sounded to herself strange and unfamiliar as she said :

'Thank you. You are very kind.'

'Then you will come?' observed Lady Hilda, who did not really want one of the party.

'No, thank you,' replied Glen, beautifully concise, for fear of being once more misunderstood.

'Why not? Probably you may never have the chance of seeing a thing of the sort again.'

This time Glen, who was getting up to boiling-point, did not vouchsafe a word.

'Say you will come, there's a good girl ;' and Lady Hilda smiled across Mr. Dawton in a manner which might, as that gentleman observed subsequently, have vanquished 'a monarch of the forest.'

'Thank you, no!' persisted Glen.

'But why won't you be good-natured?'

'We don't visit,' answered the girl, whose cheeks were literally aflame with anger.

It was too much for Lady Hilda. She burst into a peal of laughter, the sound of which dried the tears that filled Glen's eyes.

'Oh, Mr. Dawton! Oh, Mr. Dawton and Mr. What-ever-is-your-name — Kelly — can't you make something of this, " *We don't visit!*" Sweet seventeen, with the dignity of a dowager and the pride of a queen. What a funny child you are! Have I offended you? I did not mean to do so. I am sorry. Shake hands and be friends.'

But Glen did not shake hands; she only let her hand lie passive, while Lady Hilda, who had come round to where she sat, took the girl's worn glove in her own dainty fingers, and went through that ceremony of reconciliation which probably meant as little on her side as on Miss Westley's.

There was a raging fury in Glen's heart that had never stirred it before—beyond speech, beyond sign. She had but one thought—how she should get out of the office—away—any place where she should never meet this odious, ill-bred woman again.

It was when the flood was at its highest that Mr. Pierson, with the best intentions, remarked :

'Mr. Kelly is a compatriot of yours, Miss Westley, who has already won great distinction in the character of the deaf gentleman in " How's Maria ?" '

Mr. Kelly, thus honourably mentioned, bowed, and so did Glen. Then, as their eyes met, she remembered his face, and where she had seen it last.

As two strange cats might, the ' compatriots' stared at each other.

There had been but one drop wanting to fill Glen's cup of mortification to overflowing, and now that drop was supplied ; whilst on his side Mr. Kelly—who, happening to have ' got on ' a good deal since that drizzling October day, had hoped never again to behold any one of his fellow-passengers on the journey to London—felt when he recognised the girl, who was not, even after so many months of metropolitan experience, much ' to look at,' as if he had suddenly gone back in the world—

as though he had sunk from the heights of the *Galaxy* back into *gauche*, untrained, untravelled Barney Kelly, fresh from Callinacoan, who had 'amused,' forsooth ! his English audience by using that remarkably strong expression which in his belief embodied the feeling of the Saxon towards his native land.

'I have seen you before, I think,' said Glen, steadying her voice as well as she could.

'We crossed in the same boat together, I believe, to Morecambe,' he answered, speaking as unconcernedly as annoyance would let him. 'I did not know,' he added, 'you were travelling to London to try your fortune as an author.'

'She has come to set the Thames on fire,' observed Lady Hilda ; ' at least, so I gather from her admirer, Mr. Pierson.'

'I trust,' added Mr. Dawton, always restlessly anxious to put an unnecessary oar in the conversation, ' she will give us due notice when the conflagration is likely to come off.'

'I will,' said Mr. Vassett, with a decision which took his hearers by surprise, while Glen contented herself by hoping mentally Lady Hilda might then be out on the river in a boat, and determinedly rose to go.

Mr. Pierson walked by her side as far as the street door.

'You have got a manuscript for us, I see?' he remarked.

'No,' said Glen, whose feathers were still ruffled.

'Yes,' persisted the reader, laying hold of the end of the roll.

'I won't leave it,' declared Glen; 'nothing shall induce me. You would let Lady Hilda Hicks see it!'

'On my honour I will not! Muggins shall take charge of it till they are all gone. Can't you trust me, Miss Westley?'

If Miss Westley had spoken out her mind she would have answered that she could not; but to this point of candour Glen's courage refused to carry her.

'Well,' she said reluctantly, 'as you promise so faithfully'—and she gave him the manuscript as if it were some rare and precious treasure—'it is my best, Mr. Pierson,' she added, forgetting her anger for a moment, as she remembered all the merits and all the beauties and all the originality, all the fire and passion and pathos of this her youngest born,

her Benjamin ; 'it is far and away stronger
than anything I have done yet. You won't
let that hateful Lady Hilda laugh over it, will
you ?'

'No ; nobody shall see it but myself. Do
not be down-hearted, Miss Westley. We
will see your name printed in big capitals
yet.'

Spite, however, of which hopeful assurance,
before she was a fortnight older there came a
letter from Mr. Vassett, saying that, although
' the report on the manuscript she had been
good enough to leave for consideration was in
many respects favourable, he did not feel disposed to undertake its publication.'

' I still adhere,' finished Mr. Vassett, ' to
the opinion I first expressed—namely, that you
cannot yet have had sufficient experience of
life to enable you to produce a satisfactory
work. To write well, an author must have
thought much. Pardon me if my remarks
seem obtrusive. I trust you will believe they
are prompted solely by my interest in your
welfare and success.'

' What is it, Glen ?' said Mr. Westley to his
daughter, as she let her hand holding the open

letter drop with a despairing gesture to her side. 'Another refusal?'

'Yes, papa, as I expected.'

'Where does the refusal come from?' asked Mr. Lacere, who had called, as he explained, 'in passing,' to see if Mr. Westley continued to like the Bloomsbury lodgings. 'Do you mind telling me?' he went on, speaking in a tone of kind sympathy.

For answer, Glen gave him Mr. Vassett's letter to read.

'I think all these people give you great encouragement, Miss Westley,' he said.

'And I think,' observed Glen, 'that they all consider time to be of as little importance now as it must have been in the days of the patriarchs, when a few years less or more of waiting could make but little difference.'

With which petulant retort she was turning to leave the room, when Mr. Lacere noticed an expression on her father's face he had seen there and wondered at more than once before.

Doubt, anxiety, trouble, were all written on that melancholy, pensive countenance, and

something beyond — something Mr. Lacere
could not analyze or understand, but which
filled him with a pity, the cause of which he
would have felt puzzled to define.

It was then he took the first decided step
along a road the end of which he could not
see.

'Miss Westley,' he said, almost involuntarily, 'give me your manuscript. Let me try
if I cannot find a purchaser for it.'

CHAPTER VII.

A STRANGE ENCOUNTER.

A HOT, close evening in the summer of 1855. A thunderstorm brooding over London. The streets dusty and stifling; scarce a breath of air stirring: what Mr. Dawton, surveying the aspect of the heavens from one of the front gates of The Wigwam, described as ' a portentous stillness ' pervading the atmosphere.

'You had far better stop at home, Will,' he expostulated. 'Kelly, do not go yet; do stay and have a morsel of supper— the crisp lettuce and the cool lobster—and we'll ice a bottle of champagne—what say you ?'

'That I must go home,' said Mr. Kelly. 'I

have copy to finish that can't be put off even
for lettuce and lobster.'

'And I promised to turn up at Cayford's,
and I shall turn up,' added Will.

'Well, young blood, young blood—it will
have its way, sirs,' commented Mr. Dawton.
'Don't forget Friday, Kelly—just a friendly
party, you know—only a few old acquaintances—a carpet-dance—sandwiches and a
glass of wine. Arty will never forgive you
if you slight her birthday—a spoiled child—a
spoiled child—sole daughter of my house and
name.'

'Who rules the whole establishment,' said
Will, holding the gate open for his companion.
'Now, Kelly, if you are ready ;' and the pair
strode off, walking together to Westminster
Bridge, where young Dawton hailed an Atlas
'bus to convey him to Paddington, while Mr.
Kelly thoughtfully wended his way along the
Belvidere Road towards Bermondsey. It was
his invariable practice when alone to select all
the narrower and meaner thoroughfares. He
got a great deal of his ' copy ' out of the less-
frequented streets ; some papers he had written
concerning Rotherhithe and Bermondsey were

about that period attracting a good deal of attention. 'Studies from Life in Pen and Ink,' he called them ; and the editor of the *Galaxy* having intimated he preferred these sketches to stories, Mr. Kelly was considering whether he could not take a few more in other parts of the town.

It is an important element in worldly success when a man proves capable of learning from experience, and is not afraid to ask himself, 'What am I best fitted to do ?'

So far Mr. Kelly had not been able to settle this last point to his satisfaction, but he was coming to understand the conditions under which he displayed such talents as he possessed to the least advantage.

For example, he found his genius did not lie in the direction of story-telling—he was destitute of some faculty without which he felt he could never really take what Mr. Dawton described as ' a grip ' of the public. The best tale he could write would not, he felt, ' bring down the house.' He had been rejected by every magazine in London except the *Galaxy*, and he knew the only reason why his stories found admittance there was because

Jim Dawton polished them up. The younger Dawtons all possessed the knack of turning out a readable tale. In most of them there was not, as a candid friend kindly told Will, 'a mortal thing.' Nevertheless, they were airy, sparkling, and vivacious, and 'took' with the public. Just as one woman out of the costliest materials finds herself unable to construct a bonnet 'fit to be seen,' while another, the rich possessor of a scrap of silk, a bit of net, a morsel of ribbon, a few stray leaves and flowers, will manufacture as coquettish and ravishing a headgear as lover need desire to see, so not all the narrative 'stock' Mr. Kelly undoubtedly possessed could be metamorphosed by him into palatable literary soup.

'I can't tell what the deuce it is the fellow wants,' said the editor of the *Galaxy* one day to Jim Dawton, when that young gentleman, thinking, as he expressed the matter, 'Kelly could surely now be trusted to walk alone,' had handed two of Barney's tales in without 'running his eye over them.'

It was quite by chance the editor glanced at the manuscript, but when he had done so, he sent for Dawton, and taxed him with having on previous occasions retouched and almost rewritten 'that Irishman's copy.'

'And I am sure I can't imagine why you bother yourself about him,' finished the great man, ' for he'll throw you over when you have served his turn, see if he don't.'

'I think he will,' answered Jim ; ' but, bless you, we never expected he'd pay us in meal or in malt for any little thing we were able to do for him. It's a poor sort of way that, according to my fancy, some folks have of giving with one hand and holding out the other to take.'

'You will never learn sense, Dawton, I am afraid,' observed the editor gravely, at which remark Jim laughed, and said he did not know who was to teach him ; and then he took Mr. Kelly's rejected manuscripts and ' polished them up a bit,' and subsequently remarked to that individual :

' I say, old boy, don't you think it is almost time you learnt to pepper and salt your stories for yourself? I'm about tired of having all the work while you get the halfpence.'

Very innocently, Mr. Kelly inquired what his friend meant, though he knew perfectly well. After he first began to write for the *Galaxy*, a letter was directed to him at the office of that paper, which proved to be from the editor of the new opposition magazine, started by an enterprising firm immediately after the 'tremendous hit' made by the *Galaxy* with the benevolent intention of knocking that journal 'into a cocked hat.' In this epistle the editor presented his compliments to Mr. Kelly, and intimated that in case the author of 'Tidford's Pet' were disposed to contribute some short tales to the *Sceptre*, he would be glad, if possible, to meet Mr. Kelly's terms. Now, as the price Mr. Kelly received from the *Galaxy*, though about six times as much as that brilliant writer would have felt thankful to receive when he began to turn out copy for his daily bread, was so much less than he heard other men boasting they were paid, he thought he would see whether he could not do as well as they; and accordingly, without committing himself about terms, he dropped a couple of manuscripts into the editorial box, together with a note, signifying

33—2

he would do himself the honour to call on
that gentleman during the course of the
ensuing week, when, he felt no doubt, they
would be able to come to some satisfactory
arrangement.

He refrained from saying a word to Mr.
Dawton about this letter and his own answer,
being well aware that between the *Galaxy* and
the *Sceptre* a feud was raging like unto the
Montagu and Capulet business of old, and
spite of all his lately acquired experience of
literary moods and morals, he did not yet quite
understand that so far from holding him back
from spoiling the Egyptians, the Dawtons
would simply have patted him on the back and
said, ' Go in and win,' or given him, in even
more forcible words, the advice vouchsafed by
the parish priest of Callinacoan, who, after
stating from the altar steps it had come to his
knowledge that gifts of food and clothing and
money were being distributed amongst his
flock by those who, like the Pharisees, hesitated
not ' to compass sea and land to make one
proselyte, and when he is become so, make him
twofold more a child of hell than themselves,'
went on to say, 'Take what ye can get from

the heretics, my poor people—everything they
are willing to give, for God knows ye have
need of it all.'

Mr. Kelly was unable to quite realize that
though honour among thieves may be possible,
chivalry as regards editors and publishers is
usually accounted among authors as worse than
folly, and for this reason he said nothing concerning the *Sceptre,* a reticence he felt indeed
very thankful subsequently to remember he
had maintained.

All in due time he ' did himself the honour '
of calling on the editor, who was out; but the
sub, who was in, sent a message that he should
like to speak to him.

Nothing doubting, Mr. Kelly entered the
editor's room—a well-furnished, well-carpeted,
well-appointed apartment, very different from
the den at the *Galaxy.*

' Money no object,' thought Mr. Kelly com-
placently. Afterwards he learned that it is
not from the best-looking offices the largest
cheques issue.

From out of the depths of a great office-
chair, placed at the side of the table farthest
from the door, rose a small man with the palest

face and the darkest eyes and the blackest hair Mr. Kelly had ever seen.

'I sent some manuscripts here last week at Mr. Hetley's request,' said the fortunate author, after the exchange of a few words of ordinary courtesy, with the assured smile and manner of a man accustomed to acceptance ; 'I hoped to have been fortunate enough to see him.'

'He has gone away for a few days,' answered the other, 'but I know all about the matter. Pray be seated,' and with a wave of his hand he indicated a chair.

Why, he never could tell afterwards, but at that point Mr. Kelly began to feel vaguely uncomfortable. This was his first interview with an editor unblessed by the genial introduction and cheerful presence of one or other of the Dawtons.

'Your manuscripts have been carefully considered, Mr. Kelly,' said the sub, laying one out quite flat on the table as he spoke, and smoothing it gently over with the palm of his hand, an action which somehow gave the author the impression of erasing all the words, 'but I regret to say—— '

'Oh ! if you do not want them I can place

them elsewhere,' interposed Mr. Kelly, speaking in such a hurry that his words almost tripped each other up. ' I shouldn't have sent you anything of mine if you had not asked me to do so.'

' Mr. Hetley was aware of that,' answered the second in command, with unruffled composure, ' and begged me to offer his apologies for the trouble he has given you. He regrets very much indeed that he cannot make use of either of your stories.'

' Of course I bow to his decision,' observed Mr. Kelly, with a fine irony perfectly thrown away on the man he addressed—a man who understood his business thoroughly, the best ' sub' perhaps in London, ' but as a matter of curiosity I should like to be informed of the grounds on which you reject my work after having requested me to submit it.'

' Yes, Mr. Hetley felt that even for his own sake some explanation should be given. When he wrote to you he had only read " Tidford's Pet," and concluded the rest of your work would be up to the same mark. Now, Mr. Kelly, if I may say so without offence, these stories are *not* up to the same mark.'

Mr. Kelly answered, with a beautiful humility, that he was sorry his poor stories did not meet with approval. He confessed they had not seemed to him so inferior, but then no author could be considered a fair judge of his own work; and, warming to his subject, Barney threw out a general statement to the effect that he presumed there were few writers able uniformly to keep to the same standard of excellence.

Mr. Kelly had advanced a good deal in his ideas and manners since he came to London. He now talked as one having authority; who had been nursed on printer's ink and weaned on small pica ; who knew all about editors, and authors, and copy, and 'trade' jealousies and old-fashioned officialism ; for whom the 'profession' held no secret, and who knew his way blindfold through all the ins and outs of journalism.

But he was speaking to a man who for twenty years had been walking the highways and by-ways of literary life ; who, though he might be little better than a machine, still, like a machine, had come in contact with the productions of some splendid workers ; who

understood his business if he understood little
else ; and who was not to be diverted from his
argument by the great and mighty airs of even
a much more important person than the author
of ' Tidford's Pet.'

' No writer can make a greater mistake than
to play tricks with his reputation,' he remarked
sententiously, ' and upon the strength of a
later success to try to float the immature productions of an earlier period of his life. That
is what you have tried to do with us, Mr.
Kelly, and even in your own interest I am
bound to say I think you have committed an
error of judgment.'

In a moment Barney grasped the state of
the case. This man thought he had been trying to foist off on the *Sceptre* some of the
crudest of his manuscripts—the very refuse of
his labours. It was gall and wormwood to the
author to find that, wanting the Dawton light
touch, minus the few bold strokes which gave
a finish to his work, stories which had cost him
labour enough, which were indeed the very
best he had ever produced, should be accounted
unfit for anything save swift burial without
funeral honours in the nearest waste-paper

basket. He had cleverness enough to conceal
the cause of his chagrin, and answered, with a
sudden change of manner which a good deal
surprised Mr. Hetley's sub :

' I dare say you are right; and at any rate
I feel obliged for your candour. I did not
really think the tales bad myself; but, as I
said before, authors are not always the best
judges of their own work. Just at the present time I am exceedingly busy ; but after a
while I hope to be able to bring you something you will consider more satisfactory ;'
and then they had a little conversation on
general subjects, and Mr. Kelly smilingly took
his manuscripts, and they parted very good
friends.

That evening was spent by Bernard Kelly
in comparing his original manuscripts with
those manuscripts as they read in print,
after one of the Dawtons had ' run them
through.'

' I can't make it out,' he at last exclaimed.
' I can't tell how the deuce they do it,' for the
fact was, Barney had hitherto considered his
brain-children marred and deformed by the
Dawton hacking, and dressing, and shortening,

and altering. He thought his finest passages were ruthlessly deleted—that for all the beauty and pathos he had read and re-read to himself with never-failing delight to be cut out by Dawton's remorseless pen, was an indignity he could scarcely endure. Even his amusing scenes were curtailed ; and what he considered his finest efforts of humour sometimes expunged altogether, and the author had only held his peace concerning these mutilations from prudence.

Now, however, he began to see it was to this chopping and changing process he owed such success as he had secured. He did not really think his compositions improved by the merciless action of the Dawton pruning-knife— quite the contrary ; but Barney was not bigoted. His firstborn in literature was dear to him, no doubt ; but he would have sacrificed it or anything else for bread-and-cheese.

' I wish I could learn the knack of how they do it,' he reflected, referring to the ease with which any one of the Dawtons could ' touch up,' or ' knock off,' or ' boil down ' an article. ' I know twice as much as any one of them. I have read ten times as many books—and good books too. What on earth can it be they have that I want ?'

It was while this question still burned in his mind he happened one Saturday night to be passing through Hoxton while the usual market was in full swing in Pitfield Street. The sight was new to him. He went home with a vivid picture of the stalls, the flaring naphtha, the eager sellers, the anxious buyers in his mind's eye, with the quaint expressions, the curious retorts, the elbowing, the jostling, the badinage, the persuading, the huckstering, fresh in his memory ; and before he lay down to sleep he produced a graphic and taking pen-and-ink sketch of the scene.

'It is capital !' said Will Dawton. 'It only needs a dash of colour here and there. Hand it over, Kelly; that's precisely the sort of thing the *Galaxy* wants.'

In the pursuit, therefore, of that 'sort of thing,' Mr. Kelly wandered south and east through all sorts of disagreeable neighbourhoods, but he liked them. Quite honestly he said he preferred Whitechapel to Belgravia, and Ratcliff Highway to Pall Mall.

There came a time when he tired of those

neighbourhoods, and, indeed, sometimes to hear him talk now, anyone might imagine he had spent his whole life amongst the Upper Ten. For Mr. Bernard Kelly has done remarkably well for himself, and if you, reader, chance to be of those who go visiting at great houses, you will certainly some evening have the pleasure of meeting a gentleman who, from the first hour of his literary life, laid himself out to 'please the public.'

After parting from his friend he strolled idly along Belvidere Road and Upper Ground Street, got on to Bankside, and so, just as the threatened thunderstorm began, found himself in that exceedingly old-world part of London which is still existing, though probably it will not exist much longer—Clink Street. It was a place he often chose to pass through ; he liked the passage round St. Saviour's Church, and the queer little bit of covered way leading from Clink Street to St. Mary's Overy Dock.

A genuine corner of ancient London it all seemed to him as he often paused at the top of the steps to look on the one hand down on the water, and on the other to take a backward and comprehensive view of Clink Street. Now,

however, as heavy drops of rain began to fall
on the stones, he thought only of getting into
shelter, and hurried up the steps and under
the covered passage that to this day seems so
quaint a relic of times long gone by.

There were other persons there before him,
as others came after; but not very many, for
Clink Street cannot be considered a leading
thoroughfare, and is certainly not largely
affected, save by those pedestrians who either
reside or have business in the neighbourhood.

Mr. Kelly, who had a long distance still to
traverse before he reached his lodgings, and
who did not feel the slightest desire to get
wet through, managed, after a few minutes, to
secure for himself a very comfortable corner,
in which he stood warm and dry, while the
rain poured down in torrents and the thunder
pealed and the lightning played about the
river and round the tower of St. Saviour's
Church, and women with their dresses tucked
up and shawls drawn over their bonnets took
advantage of any lull in the tempest to scuttle
off through the passage, and men who had
waited till the worst of the storm was over
buttoned their coats close, turned up their

collars and the bottoms of their trousers, and
set out, to be driven again to shelter when
they reached the other side of the market.

It was getting late; the shades of evening
were closing down, and still there appeared
little chance of a storm which seemed always
' working round,' ' blowing over,' when Mr.
Kelly's attention was excited by the appearance of two men, who, in one of the short lulls
of the rain and thunder, came running up the
steps, and took advantage of the best position
they found vacant at the top.

' By George !' exclaimed the shorter of the
two, who took off his hat and mopped his forehead, and wiped the perspiration from his face,
' we are just in time, Noll. How it comes
down ! My luck all over ! Thin boots—no
overcoat, no umbrella !'

' Well, you are no worse off than I am,'
replied the other, in an oily, unctuous, persuasive voice, ' and we are in very good quarters
here ; and the rain, doubtless, will soon give
over.'

' And we'll see a rainbow in the sky, and an
angel will bring us changes of raiment, and
perhaps a carriage to convey us to our des-

tination—that's the sort of thing, ain't it ?—
your sort of thing, I mean.'

'I wouldn't, you know—I wouldn't, really,
if I was you.'

'Wouldn't you ? If you were me, you don't
know what you might do ;' and then, in a lilt-
ing sort of monotone, the first speaker went on,
'Suppose that you were I—suppose that you
were me—suppose we both were somebody
else—I wonder who it would be ? Riddle
me, riddle me ree, Noll, can you tell me
that ?'

The rain was now falling fast and furious,
and the thunder making such a din, Mr.
Kelly could not have heard any more of the
conversation for some time, even if his attention had not been distracted by the flashing
of the lightning and the noise made by the
rain as it plashed heavily into the dock
below.

For the time the corner was full, and even
the passage beyond, only partially protected
from the storm, held a fair number of people
who did not care to expose themselves to the
full violence of the tempest ; but whenever the
rain abated even a little, most of the persons

sheltering repeated the experiment of venturing forth, and once again the place became comparatively empty, though the drops still pattered down and the thunder continued to mutter angry threats from the distance, whither it had temporarily departed.

That the talk had never really ceased between the two men Mr. Kelly was aware, and now, as they drew a little nearer to him, the younger said, evidently in answer to some previous remark of his more self-possessed and decorous companion :

' I suppose you have heard, however, that at the corner of every street in London there is a capitalist waiting to be taken in ?'

' I have heard,' replied the other, ' what comes much to the same thing — namely, that every half-hour in the day a fool crosses London Bridge with a rogue following him.'

' Well, and what do you make of that ?' asked the younger man triumphantly.

' Surely there is not much to make of anything of the sort. We know there have been rogues and fools, and dupes and knaves since the beginning of time, and till our poor, im-

perfect human nature is different from what it
is——'

'Now, drop that,' interrupted the serious
man's companion ; 'you know I can't stand
preaching.'

'It was you began it——'

'Preaching! I'll swear it wasn't,' cried the
other, in such an excited tone that those persons who were still 'standing up' involuntarily
turned and looked at the pair.

Mr. Kelly found it impossible to catch the
remonstrance addressed to the younger man
by the elder ; but his words produced an
effect for a short time—not for long, though ;
every woman who furled or unfurled her
umbrella was addressed with jocular familiarity ; every man had a remark of some
sort addressed to him. There were a few
who, being wet and sulky, did not take kindly
to this chaff ; but upon the whole, pater and
mater familias and the younger lads and lasses
only laughed at the outpouring of spirit of the
'funny chap,' as Mr. Kelly mentally called
him ; and when Barney himself was addressed
as an 'old cock,' and asked whether 'the
missus would give him a wigging when he got

home for stopping out without leave,' the merriment of the audience culminated in shouts of laughter.

Stimulated by these marks of approval, the young man, with his hat pushed to the back of his head, his hands deep in his pockets, his back up against the woodwork, and his feet a little inclined to slip away from under him on their own account, proceeded to improve the occasion still further by asking whether he should 'go home first to make peace and tuck up the young ones,' a question which so delighted many ladies present that they were fain to bury their faces in their handkerchiefs, and put their hands to their sides, cast side-long glances of amusement at each other, and giggle and otherwise encourage 'the gentle-man' to proceed to greater lengths.

Which indeed he did. He found many things to say, and he said them ; he seemed in the highest, maddest mood, and treated the perpetually recurring 'I wouldn't if I was you—I wouldn't indeed,' of his mentor as a capital joke. He even attacked one staid and starched spinster with the question whether she wanted a ' nice good little boy to bring up,' because personally he felt he had 'great need of a mother's care.'

'You have great need of something, sir, I think,' she retorted, and walked away with great dignity, a handkerchief tied over her bonnet and her silk dress uplifted sufficiently to show a very neat foot and ankle, followed by such a pantomime from the young fellow of kisses wafted after her retreating form, and heart-pressing and deep sighing, and a stave of a song in admiration of 'charms he might ne'er see again,' that even Bernard Kelly, who was not easily moved to laughter, had to join the chorus of merriment which rang out from that harbour of refuge perched above the dock of St. Mary Overy.

One thing, however, Mr. Kelly noticed— that through all his folly the young man, who was called by his grave companion Lance, never seemed to lose hold of a certain thread of dialogue, to which at intervals he returned again and again. When he thus took up the original subject—whatever it might be—his face was serious enough ; then people might come or people might go without eliciting any remark save the most cursory and trivial. At such times he forgot to look about him either, though his companion did, as though uneasy lest what he said might be overheard, or anxious to get away and so end the discussion.

The author stole a glance at them both now and then, and utterly failed to arrive at any conclusion as to what they might be, till he chanced to hear the elder say :

' I can't—I assure you what you ask is not within my power to do. I am only temporarily associated with a religious society, and——'

' O Lord !' broke in the other ; ' talk about Saul among the prophets—what's that to Noll Butterby ?'

' Hold your tongue, do !' remonstrated Noll angrily. ' Why will you talk so loud ? People can hear all you say, and——'

Here he dropped his voice so low that even Bernard Kelly, who was standing near, could not catch the remainder of the sentence, to which Lance replied in a much less exalted tone than that he usually employed.

He was but little over twenty, Mr. Kelly decided ; so thin that he really looked as if he

had not an ounce of flesh on his bones—a restless, electrical sort of being, who could not
have kept still or silent had he been paid for
doing so, possessed of a temperament that
would never let him get even moderately fat.
He was wiry, but not muscular; certainly no
athlete, Barney—who knew a good deal about
men who hunted, and boated, and walked, and
jumped, and fought, and played at cricket—
felt very sure. His thin, straight hair, which
he was constantly pushing upwards with nervous, bony fingers, hovered between the con-
fines of bright yellow and dark red; his
complexion was muddy, his expression
anxious; his eyes were small, and of a
greyish-blue, and as a rule ranged from
object to object with the same quick, jerky
uncertainty that characterized all his movements.

'Mad,' thought Mr. Kelly; and then he
amended his phrase, 'drunk.' Yet for a man
not sober he was wonderfully fluent; he never
stopped for a word; he went right on with a
flow of language Barney had seldom heard
equalled except by a ' Cheap Jack.'

On the whole, he more resembled a ' Cheap

Jack' with a slight knowledge of literature
added to his other stock-in-trade than anything else; and as the rain, though still
coming down pretty steadily, was not nearly
so heavy as it had been, Mr. Kelly might have
gone away to Bermondsey satisfied the young
fellow followed the occupation in question, or
at all events one analogous to it, had he not,
to his astonishment, suddenly heard him break
out with this:

'How did I first get to know the Dawtons?
and why did I break with them? I don't mind
telling you or any man. I have nothing to
be ashamed of in the matter, have I?'

And he turned on Barney, who, in the excess
of his astonishment, was staring at him with
all his might.

'Unless I knew what you were talking
about, I really could not venture to give an
opinion,' answered Mr. Kelly, with diplomatic
reticence.

'You're Scotch, ain't you?' cried out the
other. 'I am sure you are. You are
Scotch!'

'Something of that sort,' agreed Barney
carelessly.

' I could have taken my affidavit of it.	You
see, Noll, he won't reply straightforwardly even
to the simplest question.	Never mind, I like
the look of you.	Jew or Gentile, I can always
tell when a man is a good sort by one glance
in his face.	My friend here wants to hear
how I fell in with a certain family, and why I
fell out with them.	I don't mind telling him,
or you, or anybody.	When a man hasn't done
anything wrong, though he is a bit down on
his luck——'

' I wouldn't, Lance—I wouldn't indeed, if I
were you.'

' If you don't quit that parrot-cry I'll wring
your neck for you,' interposed Lance, with an
expression of the most perfect amiability, ' or
chuck you into the sewer there—our noble
Thames is nothing but a common sewer.	Here,
you, sir, why have you shrunk back into your
corner ?	Come here ; or, better still, I'll edge
up to you.'

And, suiting his action to his word, he
moved close beside Mr. Kelly, and laid one
hand on that gentleman's shoulder, while with
the other he drew the reluctant Butterby into
conclave while he said :

'Oh! you need not be making signs and tokens to him about me. I know very well what I am doing and saying. If you keep as cool a head among your religious folks as I have now, you'll get on, never fear. Do you happen to know,' he added, addressing Bernard Kelly, '*who stole the squire's apples?*'

'No, I don't,' answered Barney, laughing; ' do you?'

' Yes, I know, bless you! but never mind that now; we were not talking about apples or the squire, but about me and the Dawtons. Did you ever meet any of them?' he stopped to inquire.

' I have heard of a Mr. Dawton, an actor, if that's the man you mean.'

' That's the man—does old fathers and heavy swells; awful muff on the stage, I think, and a far greater bore in private life. But that's nothing. You are not a friend of his, are you?'

' I! How should I be a friend of his?'

' I didn't think you were; you are out of that sort of beat altogether; but still, it is as well to be careful. No, I am not going to hold my tongue, Noll. However, as I was saying, Dawton's an awful bore, but he did not behave half badly to me. He was good to me—I'll say that for him ; and so was his wife, so were the sons, and so was everybody—only—well, I was a fool ; you are not surprised to hear that, are you ?'

'Of course he is not,' remarked Mr. Butterby. 'Why should anybody be who hears you talking about your private affairs in this way ?'

'I did not ask your opinion, and I am not such a fool as I look, as some persons may find out before they are much older. I do not say I have done as well as you, Mr. Noll ; but the end is not yet, and while you are still plodding through the highways and byways, distributing tracts, you need not be surprised to see me driving past in my carriage. Should you like to hear how I came to London without a shoe to my foot ?'

'Well, I don't know,' answered Mr. Kelly, thus once more appealed to; 'this is scarcely a place to pass the night, and——'

'Ah, you are laughing at me ! You mean I'd keep you talking till morning. No, I wouldn't. I wonder somebody doesn't start a bar in this corner. What I'd give now just for the least taste of Scotch whisky! We'd have that in compliment to you. Dawton was the fellow to lap; that's how he got himself out of all his engagements. Couldn't keep his nerves steady; got maudlin, too, at times. If drink hurts a man, he ought to take the pledge —" Taste not, touch not." What are you grinning at ?' he asked suddenly. ' I suppose you are thinking, " Physician, heal thyself;" but you are out—quite wrong. Bless you, I don't drink! I haven't the chance. I only wish I had! You can't get drunk unless you have money, or tick, or friends; and I have neither money, nor tick, nor friends, and all because of a young woman—such a trim little craft, such a pretty, clever creature! She might have made a man of me; but never mind, when I am riding in that carriage I was telling you about,' and he nodded to Mr. Butterby, ' she'll be sorry she's not sitting at my side!'

' Perhaps you may make up your quarrel,' suggested Mr. Kelly.

' Oh no! I am not one of your forgiving

sort. I have no notion of huffing to-day and kissing to-morrow. So far as I am concerned, Miss Arty will have all her life to repent in.'

'Who is Miss Arty?' asked Mr. Kelly, as innocently as though he had not seen a young lady of that name a couple of hours previously.

'Old Dawton's daughter. She does not take after him, though.'

' And she wouldn't have anything to do with you, Lance?' said Mr. Butterby.

' It was this way, you see. She did not seem able to forget how poor I was when she first set eyes on me—*they* had the bailiffs in at the time for that matter, and so I reminded her. I told her I meant to be a big fellow yet, that I knew I had it in me to ' make a splash,' that all I wanted was a wife to keep me steady, that I would win a fortune for her ; but she didn't see it, or she wouldn't see it. She said she thought we had better wait till I had got part of the fortune, at any rate. I declared I would do nothing of the kind, that if she liked she could have me then, but that if she did not choose to take me as I was, she might do the other thing.'

'And so?' ventured Mr. Kelly, as the rejected suitor paused.

'She did the other thing,' explained Lance. 'I put it quite plainly to her. I said, "Remember, I am not going to come begging and praying to you to reconsider your decision. I have made you a fair offer, but I will not make it to you again. It must be now or never."

'"Then I am afraid it must be never,"' she answered, as coolly as you please. That was a way to treat a fellow who worshipped the ground she walked on, who would have dressed her in satins and velvets if he could, who thought there was nobody like her in the world. It's no matter, though; I am not going to break my heart because a woman's false. When I think of the walks we used to take over Battersea Fields, I—— But she'll be sorry some day, won't she?'

'I dare say she is sorry now,' observed Mr. Kelly soothingly.

'No, she's not. She won't feel much sorrow till she hears a great talk about me, and people saying: "What a clever fellow that Lance Felton must be! Why, he came to London with scarcely a shoe to his foot, and look at him now—he's rolling in wealth!" '

'There's some work cut out for you before anybody can say that about Lance Felton with any truth,' remarked Mr. Butterby, with a saintly sneer.

'And to enable him to do the work cut out,' exclaimed Mr. Kelly, 'I propose, now the rain is abating a little, that we adjourn to the nearest tavern and drink to his success in the best "Scotch" we can get.'

'I knew you were the right sort,' cried Lance with enthusiasm. 'Oh yes, I can always tell with the most cursory——'

'Never mind that now,' interrupted Bernard Kelly. 'Come along!' and, thus exhorted, Mr. Felton, as he expressed the matter, 'toddled.'

The tide of improvement which has for the last fifteen years been setting steadily through modern Babylon and converting London from the ugliest and most interesting city in the world, into the handsomest and most hopelessly commonplace, could not, of course, when it was sweeping better things into the limbo of forgetfulness, be expected to spare so insignificant a tavern as the old-fashioned public-house to which Mr. Kelly and his companions repaired for that modicum of Scotch whisky which was, so said Mr. Felton, to be ordered in honour of his new acquaintance's nationality. To Bernard Kelly his nationality had become a matter of the most supreme indifference. He was not a man likely to gush about 'old Ireland' and Brian Boroihme. Erin's harp, and Erin's shamrock, and Erin's wrongs, were mere phrases which conveyed even less meaning to his mind than they could possibly have done to the 'falsest' Saxon in the whole of England. If anyone had asked him then his views on the vexed question of Irish policy, he would have confessed to entertaining none. He was not eager to flourish his native land in the face of the tyrant. He had found a country full of leeks and cucumbers, and fleshpots and money, and he meant to adapt himself to its manners and customs, as far as possible.

Supposing it pleased people to take him for a Scotchman, well and good—he would not undeceive them. He had learnt at a very early period of his metropolitan experiences that the native of any other land—Jew, Greek,

Pole—was more acceptable to the English mind than an Irishman, and consequently he did not now go about the world proclaiming that he claimed Callinacoan as his birthplace, as he might once have done. He had heard quite enough of that sort of thing from Miss Bridgetta Cavan to warn him off the subject for ever. Beggars in rags and tatters Mr. Donagh's aunt was wont to greet with delight as having been, like herself, born in the Emerald Isle, and accustomed to potatoes boiled in their jackets. Not a man, woman, or child with whom she came in contact round and about West Ham and Stratford did she suffer to remain in ignorance of her Irish extraction.

When she haggled over the price of a fowl, she told the dealer she could have got a ' far better one ' for sixpence at Callinacoan ; and the same information was vouchsafed concerning every other necessary of life, were the matter in hand a ' hank ' of worsted or the ' smoothing ' of Mat's immaculate shirt-fronts.

With a considerable amount of ostentation Mr. Lance Felton, producing a crown-piece, which he loudly declared he would tell no man how he became possessed of, insisted on 'standing treat.'

Closely watching him, Mr. Kelly could see that crown-pieces had not been plentiful in the young man's pocket. From the way he flung the coin down on the counter it almost seemed as though he were challenging the resources of the house to produce sufficient change.

'H'm,' thought Mr. Kelly; and when the whisky was brought in a measure instead of in the fair and simple shape of 'outs,' to which the liberal-minded youth had evidently been most accustomed, Barney—the liquor having been first passed to him ' out of compliment '— poured into his glass a quantity which made both his companions stare.

'Come, I say—you know,' expostulated Mr. Felton; 'leave other fellows a chance, do. I did not mean you to take *quite* all.'

'Oh! there's enough left for you,' answered Barney carelessly. 'English heads are more easily upset than ours. However, let us have another measure. I don't care to drink my grog as weak as tea.'

'Well, you must be a seasoned vessel,' exclaimed Mr. Felton, as, not without admira-

tion, he noted the exceedingly moderate quantity
of water Mr. Kelly mixed with his potations.
' Why, if I was to take that——'

Mr. Kelly smiled meaningly.   He knew
very well why this youngster's hand was unsteady, and his talk rambling, and his eye un-
settled, and his tongue indiscreet.

' Yes,' he decided ; ' my lad, you began with
the bottle betimes.   You have had a touch of
D. T. already, or I am much mistaken.   Unless
you mind what you are about, things won't go
well with you.'   But he spoke no word of this
aloud ; he only sipped his own fiery draught,
and laughed inwardly to see how young Felton
was all unconsciously following Mat Donagh's
lead, and adopting the course people learned
in the ways and customs of drunkenness assert
conducts to swift and sure destruction, viz.,
adding spirit to the top of the tumbler, instead
of conscientiously depositing it in the bottom.

Few men living probably knew more about
the vice of intemperance than Bernard Kelly.
He had seen every form, he thought, of in-
toxication before he set foot in England ; but
once in London, he found he had still a great
deal to learn.

He felt quite interested in watching his two companions: Noll, who it seemed to him could himself have drunk a quart and walked away as steadily afterwards as if he had never tasted a drop; and Felton, who was, he felt convinced, already a confirmed tippler, and to whose nervous and excitable nature stimulants were evidently a swift and sure poison.

Strange to say, Kelly had, since he quitted Abbey Cottage, well-nigh become a practical, though not professed teetotaler.

It needed no prophet to foretell the probable result likely to ensue from the habits into which Mat Donagh and Mr. Dawton had fallen.

Nothing except a miracle, thought Barney, could save either from eventual bankruptcy and degradation. He knew what his father had sunk into; he had seen others well-off, lose lands, and houses, and character, simply because they lacked self-control, because the demon of drink took possession of them and turned every good angel that had hitherto dwelt in their bosoms adrift. This was not a form of temptation he had expected to find waiting for him in London; but as he did meet it, he determined it should not ruin his future.

He drank nothing at home, and no more out than seemed to his mind necessary, unless he had a purpose to serve in assuming the semblance of good-fellowship. If Mr. Bernard Kelly liked he could tell to-day of many a noble craft, laden with the treasures of genius, he has seen go down engulfed in seas of champagne and burgundy—to say nothing of those more prosaic destroyers, brandy, and rum, and gin—but he would not. Mr. Kelly is now above all things respectable, no man better understands the wisdom of silence—the beauty of accepting things as they seem to be rather than as they are.

He would not amend the doctor's certificate for any consideration—conventional phrases are eternally on his lips. He has never written a line posterity need desire to read, yet he sits high above the clamour of struggling authorship a successful man !

Standing in front of the bar of the old public-house, Mr. Felton was kind enough to enlighten all within hearing as to his own opinions, talents, and antecedents. From the

period when he went to a dame school to have
the alphabet beaten into him, to that present
hour in which he had made the acquaintance
of his new friend, he spared no incident which
seemed for the moment important to his wandering brain. He was as discursive as Barnaby
Rudge, and to Mr. Kelly he did not seem much
wiser. True, his folly was dashed with a vein
of shrewdness, which shone occasionally across
his discourse like the flash of a lantern through
the darkness of night. But Barney had grown
very weary of him, utterly tired of his awful
egotism, and was just considering how he
could manage to slip him off, when Noll, whose
eyes were no brighter, and face no ruddier, and
tongue no looser for all the whisky he had
swallowed, said in that aggravatingly slow
voice of his :

'Now, Lance, if I'm to see you home it is
time we were moving.'

'I don't want you to see me home,' cried
Lance indignantly. 'I can see myself home
without any help.'

'No, you can't,' was the calm reply ; 'you'll
get locked up, or you'll lie down on some doorstep and catch your death of cold ; or——'

'You go home yourself; go to Jericho, if you like. You'll come with me to my crib, won't you?' went on Lance, appealing to Barney Kelly.

'Well, I don't know,' answered the latter; 'it all depends upon where your crib may be. For instance, I won't go back with you to Hammersmith, or Tottenham, or—— '

'Oh! I'm not particular,' interposed the other; 'I'll take a shakedown wherever you live, and welcome.'

'Couldn't possibly oblige you in that way,' said Mr. Kelly; 'I reside with my grand-mamma, a most particular old lady—bedroom candlesticks brought in at half-past ten, all lights out at eleven. She would disinherit me on the spot if I introduced such a wild spirit as you to her.'

'What's the matter with me?' asked Mr. Lance Felton, a little thickly.

'A good deal, I think. You had better take your friend's advice, and get home as soon as you can. I'll set you a good example, and be off.'

But Lance would not have the knot thus

cut ; he bade Noll take a Brixton 'bus, and said plainly :

' It is no use your waiting for me.'

A very demon of contradiction seemed raised within him, and while with one hand he persistently pointed Noll to the door, with the other he clung to Mr. Kelly, who at length, in order to pacify his excitement and avoid a scene the landlord's looks seemed in anticipation to deprecate, promised to take care of him.

It was quite fine when they all left the tavern ; a delightful coolness had succeeded to the heat of the earlier part of the evening ; the stars were shining overhead ; and though the pavement under foot was wet, the heavy rain had so completely washed the thoroughfares, that walking seemed what it rarely is in London—an absolute pleasure.

' Which way ?' asked Bernard Kelly, as they stood waiting to know what it might please Mr. Felton to do next.

' Wait a minute,' answered the younger man. ' We'll see Noll into a 'bus first. I'm not going to have you prowling after us,' he added, rudely addressing his friend.

'I wouldn't speak in that way if I were you,' said Noll, resorting to his accustomed formula.

'I'll speak any way I like, without asking your leave ; you may depend upon that,' retorted Lance.

'Then I may as well cross over,' remarked his friend, with unruffled composure ; and suiting the action to the word, he picked his way deliberately to the other side, where he took up his position, waiting for the Brixton omnibus to make its appearance.

'We won't go till we see him fairly off,' said Lance, who still, perhaps for prudential reasons, kept a firm hold of Bernard Kelly's arm. 'He is as deep as a draw-well; he would follow us in a minute.'

'What would it matter if he did?' asked Barney, who was beginning to wish himself well rid of his companion.

'It mightn't matter to you,' answered Lance, 'but I don't choose him to know anything about *me*. He is a mean, close, dangerous, double-faced cur, that is what he is, if you want to know, and he *did* steal the squire's apples !'

'Well, suppose he did; there was no great sin in that, was there? Most boys steal squires' apples when they can get a chance.'

'Ay! but he wasn't a boy, and he let somebody else get the blame of it.'

'Oh!' said Mr. Kelly, beginning to see light.

'He's a cad! that's what he is; now, when he could make a bit of amends, he won't. His old aunt died awhile ago, and left him £600. A clever fellow might make his fortune with a quarter of that. There's the 'bus—full inside —oh! he's getting up on the knifeboard—see him? Now we may get along.'

'I hope we haven't very far to go,' remarked Barney, who felt his companion leant far too heavily on his arm, and heard with dismay his speech becoming thicker and less articulate.

'Not far—don't be afraid, I know my way —stop a minute, and let's look at the lights in the water.'

'No, no; come on, do!' entreated Mr. Kelly. 'It is getting late, and I want to get home. You can look at the lights any other night.'

Never before had London Bridge seemed so long to him; never before did the City, to his eye, wear so deserted and dreary an aspect.

'If I only knew where the drunken idiot lived,' he considered, 'I should not so much care; but I doubt very much if he is in a state to get safe there.'

He did not overrate the point of inebriation at which Lance had arrived, but he greatly underrated the clearness of that young gentleman's mind, even at times when his limbs were particularly unsteady. Though his talk was rambling, a thread of connected sense ran through it. The main facts Mr. Kelly gathered from his desultory conversation were that he had a special spite against 'Noll;' that, indeed, he had a spite against most people; that he felt a fervent admiration for, and envy of, a large number of persons whom he vaguely designated as 'swells;' that he had the greatest desire possible to 'ride in his carriage' and 'splash' those who had shown him 'the cold shoulder;' that he entertained unlimited confidence in his own abilities; that he had very little belief in the cleverness of anybody else; that he hoped Miss Arty would live to regret having turned up her nose at him; that he meant to marry very soon, if only to show he had no notion of wearing the willow ; that he knew a girl who worshipped the ground he walked on, and was worth a thousand—aye, a hundred thousand—of Dawton's daughter. He was not always perfectly audible, and he was very often wholly unintelligible, but the impression he left on Bernard Kelly's mind was that Miss Arty might consider herself well rid of her lover, for that no weaker, vainer, more vindictive, less reliable young fellow ever reeled home to bed.

It may be said at once that the sight of this extraordinary suitor—who, even according to his own account, had sprung from the people— increased the determination Mr. Kelly formed at a very early stage of their acquaintance of getting out of the Dawton set as soon as he felt strong enough to do without their assistance.

He was fast getting into a maze of speculations concerning the Dawtons' antecedents and his own chances of success in the future, when he felt himself suddenly pulled up, and Lance came to a full stop at the door of an old house in a narrow and dirty City lane.

' Here we are,' said the young man, lurching

heavily against his companion as he began searching for the latch-key.

'What do you mean? Is this where you live?'

'It is where I lodge. Come in, and you'll see how I'm treated—worse than any dog; enough to make a fellow with brains shoot himself—or somebody else.'

Seeing that the shaking fingers could not succeed in their search, Mr. Kelly coolly put his own hand in Lance's pocket and extracted the key. Throwing open the door, they stepped into a wide hall, where a gas-jet was burning.

'Now, where are we to go?' asked Barney, who felt a weight lifted off his mind. 'Upstairs?'

For answer Lance only shook his head.

'It's in here I stop,' he said, indicating a room on the left hand, in which also there seemed a light.

'Well, this is a queer adventure, too,' decided Mr. Kelly, as he stood inside a bare, meagrely furnished office, which contained little beyond two counters running at right angles, a stool, a desk, and a chair.

Some maps were hanging on the walls, which were likewise embellished with shipping bills representing imposing-looking vessels in full sail.

'I may leave you now, I suppose,' said Mr. Kelly, drawing a deep breath of relief.

'What's the hurry? Wait a minute, and then you can turn out the gas for me.'

'But you don't sleep here?' looking round in search of any possible couch and perceiving none.

'Don't I! You'll soon see. I told you I was treated worse than a dog, and I am. And he makes a great merit of what he does for me, too; thinks, I suppose, I ought to be grateful to him for his charity. Well, time, they say, proves all things. Here's a nice, comfortable bed for a man to turn into;' and, suiting the action to the word, Mr. Lance Felton with much difficulty got down on his knees, and then, without the ceremony of dismantling himself of any article of dress—not even his hat, which, however, tumbled off, apparently of its own accord, he rolled under the counter and disappeared from Mr. Kelly's sight.

In astonishment too great for words Barney
surveyed this proceeding ; then, peeping over
the counter, he beheld the youth's prostrate
figure extended on some sacks, over which was
laid a piece of baize.

'By-by,' murmured Lance. 'I'm dead beat,
I think. You'll come and look me up soon,
won't you ?'

'Oh yes,' answered Bernard Kelly, who,
however, had not the faintest intention of
doing anything of the kind.

'And turn down the gas, will you, and shut
the door, to keep out that —— old house-
keeper !'

'All right,' replied Mr. Kelly. 'Good-night,
and pleasant dreams.'

Then he closed the door, as requested, but
paused for a moment in the hall to read the
names which were painted on the wall.

Second floor.—Duncombe and Co.

First floor.—M. Logan Lacere.

Ground floor. — Lacere Bros., Shipping
Agents.

'It's a strange world,' thought Mr. Bernard
Kelly, as he retraced his steps across London
Bridge, and thence wended his way to Ber-

mondsey; and indeed it is, the strangest thing about it being that, wide as the world seems, we find it practically so small we are always jostling and running up against each other.

CHAPTER VIII.

NED'S LETTER.

DOWN in the Valley of the Thames, on the Middlesex side of the river, but quite away from the water—among the moors that give a character of such peculiar loneliness to that little-known part of the country—the Westleys had found for themselves a small cottage ; and, remote from London, Glenarva, in a silence that after the hum of the busy streets made her ears ache, and in a solitude by comparison with which Ballyshane might have been accounted a populous city, was trying to write another novel.

At first she did not find it easy work ; the absence of all mental excitement, the utter

stillness, broken only by the songs of the
birds and the bleating of sheep, the flat and to
her most uninteresting landscape, the lack of
young companionship, depressed her for a time
beyond measure—bowed her spirit down to the
very earth. But this did not last for long.
After a few weeks her imagination took root
in this fresh soil, and wound itself round desolate tracts of stretching moorland intersected
by sluggish streams, and twined fanciful wreaths
about domains where the grounds were wild
and neglected, and startled deer bounded
across parks that there seemed no owner to
enjoy. Had she known all about these places,
the explanation of their unregarded appearance
might have proved prosaic enough, but as
matters stood she found abundant scope for
fancy, and ignorant of everything connected
with the men and women who some day meant
to return and live in those great deserted
mansions, she made up stories for herself of
wrong and sorrow and sin and suffering. It
was about that time Glen began to find writing
harder work than she had ever previously conceived it could become. She did not suffer
now from that trouble which had startled and

perplexed her when she first arrived in London
—the absence of ideas.   Plots and characters
she soon found came almost unbidden ; but
her difficulty was to mould them into shape,
to fit the different pieces of her puzzle together,
so as to form an intelligible whole, to make
her people lifelike, to show them doing simple
things in a simple manner, and talking as men
and women do talk in real life, and not as they
so often talk in books.

Sometimes the girl lost heart altogether ;
her thoughts were so vast, her power of expressing them so small! It cost her more trouble
to write a single chapter of that book than it
had done previously to produce a whole
volume.   Quite unconsciously to herself she
was passing out of the mere rudimentary stage
of authorship into its higher branches, and no
one stood beside her desk to explain she was
not retrograding but progressing, that the
reason she found writing now so hard was not
because any virtue of genius had departed from
her, but because the discipline which alone could
make her writings worth reading had begun.

The sadness of the landscape also sometimes
oppressed her very soul.   It lacked all life and

animation and cheerfulness—flat fields, stretching commons destitute of gorse and heather,
slowly flowing water, more like dykes than
rivulets, bordered by mournful pollards, and
only enlivened by the occasional presence of
a party of ducks; farmhouses at distant
intervals, a few cottages scattered here and
there, wide roads where once coaches passed
constantly, now totally deserted ; no station
within three miles, and only about four trains a
day to town ; few inhabitants above the rank of
labourers, and those there were perfectly unable to comprehend why Mr. Westley and his
daughter should have selected such an out-of-
the-way corner of the world to live in—a non-
resident rector, a curate and his wife, who
were very kind and friendly, but who evidently could not quite understand the position
of these new parishioners—altogether a strange
experience for Glenarva, who did not perhaps
take very kindly to the place or the people,
and who was regarded by them as a perfect
enigma, keeping herself to herself as she did,
taking long solitary walks, and generally maintaining a dignified seclusion from which she
never willingly emerged.

For some reason best known to the local
wisdom of the village, popular opinion soon
decided that Mr. Westley was engaged in a
lawsuit which had brought him over from
Ireland, and kept him till it was settled chained
near London.   The many letters and the large
packets of papers were thus satisfactorily
accounted for, and even the few journeys Glen
took to town were assigned to the same cause.
' Mr. Westley, poor gentleman! being in weak
health, of course his daughter had to see to
the business for him.'

Mr. Westley was in weak health, and his
daughter, as is usual in such cases, seemed the
only person who failed to realize the fact ;
indeed, it might have been hard enough for a
much older individual who had always lived
with the once owner of Glenarva to comprehend he was less strong than usual.

Always delicate, always, save by fits and
starts, limp mentally, from the day he saw his
grand castle begin to totter, Mr. Westley sank
into the condition of an invalid.   He had at
first nothing whatever in a physical sense
wrong with him.   The mournful tone of his
voice, the languor of his movements, his dis-

like to anything which brought him into contact with his fellows, arose not from illness, but the utter collapse of hope. Had he been a stronger man, he must either have died or gone out and fought fortune again—again, perhaps, to lose ; but in any case he would have made another bid for success.

As matters were, he simply sank without a struggle—unless, indeed, the feeble effort he made on first returning to London to recall the fact of his existence to one former friend could be termed a struggle. His worldly affairs got gradually worse and worse, while he himself, with, as has been said, nothing really wrong as regarded his health, sank into the condition of a confirmed invalid.

He did not walk, or work, or ride, or boat, or visit. People accepted the fact of his illness and incapacity without troubling themselves to consider what was the matter with him.

He had no intention of posing for a martyr, or crying ' Wolf;' and yet in effect it was owing to his constant depression and gentle inactivity that Glen, when disease really laid its hand upon him, failed utterly to see what was happening.

Mr. Westley knew, however. With the silence of love, he kept his knowledge to himself, but he was perfectly well aware that at last a mortal ailment had fastened upon him, and that though the course it pursued might be slow, the end would prove fatally sure.

Then it was at the eleventh hour he began to reproach himself, to consider what he might have done, if he had but possessed sufficient energy. During the long summer days, when Glen was writing or out walking, when she was thinking, planning, hoping for the future, he sat, with the scent of the simple flowers growing about their little dwelling filling the humble sitting-room, anxiously considering his daughter's life, which ere many years he knew would have to be lived without him, and reproaching himself for not having in the past done something which it was absolutely impossible a person of his temperament ever could at any time have accomplished.

To say that a man might have done this or that had he been more energetic seems about as sensible as to suggest he might have written an opera or an epic poem, or painted a picture, or built St. Paul's, or tunnelled the Alps, without the genius for compassing any one of these feats being conferred upon him by nature.

To have asked Mr. Westley to go out into the world and fight among the rank-and-file was like asking a lame man to run, or a deaf man to hear, or a blind man to see! After he first left Glenarva he had thought to insure his life, but, perhaps without any sufficient reason, the doctor gave so doubtful a report of his constitution that the money asked in the way of premium could not be considered other than prohibitory.

Then he strove to put by a little, and in effect did manage, by dint of the most painful economy and beautiful self-denial, to fill a small purse for a rainy day—or for Glen, when days with him were past for ever.

On this amount he had tried not to encroach, keeping it in a bank where he got low interest, but felt his small store safe. The money Mr. Merritt had contrived to get him before he left Ballyshane was pretty well expended.

He and Glen had lived close—painfully close—but as it was impossible for them to limit their expenses to the trifling sum which sufficed at Ballyshane, somehow pence had gone, and then shillings, and then pounds, and the sovereigns laid aside for 'extras' dwindled down, till at length but few remained to give a sense of strength and security to the regular income, which was far—far too limited.

Nevertheless, Mr. Westley was not uneasy —not very uneasy, that is to say. As the guineas went, his conviction on the subject of Glen's ability to earn money grew. He had substantial reasons for this belief. Mr. Pedland's mind was at length made up to bring out Miss Westley's novel in the autumn, while through Mr. Lacerc's intervention one of the best publishing houses had been induced to accept the great work Mr. Vassett felt it 'would be inexpedient for him to produce,' and Mr. Lacere believed she was to receive some small sum for the copyright.

If these good things had come to Glenarva at Ballyshane, if a five-pound note had dropped out of a publisher's letter while she was within sound of the wash of the Atlantic waves, the girl would have gone mad with joy; but now, though she was glad and thankful, she did not feel elated, as might once have been the case. The first meagre course of success was announced, but its advent had been so long delayed the girl's eager appetite was gone. She had been trying to reach the grapes for such a time that she felt too weary and jaded to eat now she was assured they were within her grasp. She was strangely quiet about the matter, her father considered. Even Mr. Lacere, who did not know her nature so well, felt surprised she failed to evince more pleasure when he cautiously broke the news of victory to her.

He and she talked about it all one evening as they paced slowly back from evening service at an old-world church to which Mr. Westley had said his daughter would accompany Mr. Lacere if that gentlemen wished to see a quaint building. The Westleys' new friend found his way sometimes down to the remote corner of the world where they were living; he discovered charms in the neighbourhood and beauties in the cottage Glen had never done; he partook of the tea she poured out as though it were some rare and expensive beverage the like of which he had never tasted except under Mr. Westley's roof; he watched

Glen as she flitted about the room, and listened
to her father's conversation as if the whole
world could hold for him no higher delight
than the society of a young girl and a man
whose name was writ large in the black books
of Fortune.

Mr. Westley liked him greatly ; he looked
forward to his visits with as much pleasure as
anything in those summer days could afford
him ; he had a vague intention of sooner or
later taking Mr. Lacere into his confidence,
telling him how utterly alone Glen must stand
when she lost her father, and entreating on her
behalf the good offices of this grave, shy man,
who under an apparently stern manner hid a
warm heart, for the daughter he would, ere she
was very much older, have to leave.

But precipitancy, except when he ought to
have been cautious, had never proved one of
Mr. Westley's besetting sins, and so he deferred and deferred the confidence till there
was no necessity to make it.

All this time Glenarva herself was not very
well, while Mr. Westley had often of late
caught what he called a chill. If he had
styled these attacks by any other name, his

daughter might have felt more uneasy than she did, but an illness which can be attributed to cold, and yields apparently to a day's rest in bed and a few simple remedies, is not one calculated to arouse keen apprehension.

It never certainly occurred to Glen to feel uneasy, though she was often depressed.

Even when Death knocks at the door, there is nothing much more difficult to realize than that one who has been with us always will talk with us no more ; that we shall never again— never till we ourselves have passed to that land which is to us now all silence and all mystery—hear the familiar voice, see the familiar face, touch the familiar hand ; that solitary and desolate, we, who never thought the word 'loneliness' could for us have a practical meaning, must labour till the evening, work till the gathering shadows tell us the day is well nigh spent and the night close at hand.

And Glenarva Westley found it just as difficult then to conceive of mortal sickness crossing their threshold as she did afterwards to realize the coming of that one visitor who may not be denied admittance.

Once, indeed, when she had sat up very late

beside the fire which that 'chill' necessitated being lighted in her father's room, a terror for which she could in nowise account seized her; and moved by some secret instinct, she crossed the room softly, and stood beside the bedside, listening to the regular breathing which told that sleep had at last come brooding gently down on Mr. Westley's eyelids. She looked at him as he lay, his features in utter repose, his arm thrown out over the coverlet, his hand half closed and still as possible. Unbidden tears rolled down her cheeks as she gazed; the whole of his wrecked life, the sadness and pathos and misery of it all, seemed for a moment more than she could endure, and when she went back to her seat and watched the leaping firelight, she wondered, with no triumphant feeling of success, but a trembling marvel, whether such blessing might be hers, she should indeed be able to make his future better than his past had been, to get all those good things for him in the days to come he had been forced to do without through the many long days that were past.

Upon another night, too, when she could not get to sleep till the early dawn of the summer's

morning stole into her room, the same un-
reasoning terror shook the girl's very soul : it
was no tangible fear which came and laid its
cold hand upon her heart, which drew her out
of bed and caused her to throw wide her
window, and, leaning over the sash, try to find
solace in the voices of the night.

How weird, and solemn, and strange they
sounded as she stood in the silence and the
semi-darkness all alone. If there be any truth
in the idea that the trouble we shall have to
pass through is faintly indicated in our imagi-
nations, as it is said the shape of the fern is
seen in miniature if we cut across its stem,
Glen then beheld as in a glass darkly the form
of the spectre she was going forward to meet.

But with the sun and the morning light, and
the thousand happy sounds of day, the horror
faded away, and Glen did not think much
more of it than she might of a bad dream.

Nevertheless she sometimes marvelled,
'Why is it I do not feel more elated at my
success ? Why do I not dance and sing with
delight ? Why am I not inclined to ask all
the world to share my joy ?'

The reason, if she could have known it, perhaps was that she did not herself believe in the success which had come. Like David when he told Ahimaaz to 'turn aside,' and waited for the tidings Cushi was bearing to him, she had a trembling presentiment that there was news to follow the announcement of her victory which should quench the shout of exultation with the bitter cry of mourning.

And for her, then, there was not even to be more than that gleam of hope which her own hand darkened. As a rule, when youth sees, or thinks it sees, the winning-post just ahead, some friend or foe walking across the course destroys the chances of success that had seemed absolute certainties. Later on, circumstances often perform this act of fouling; but in the outset of life it is generally a human being who, from a love of marring and meddling and proffering unasked-for advice, and gossiping about matters which concern no person save the racer pushing onward to the goal, affects the results of the struggle, and sometimes changes the whole course of existence.

It was an apparently slight cause that prevented the great house bringing out Glen's novel; the check came suddenly, and in the form of a letter from Ned Beattie.

As was her usual practice, the girl, always an early riser, had walked across the fields to meet the postman. No more lovely morning ever dawned. In the woods the doves were cooing ; high above head the larks sang loud and clear; over the distant moor hung a purple haze—a sure sign of heat ; down by the watercourses the cattle were standing knee-deep in the stream, or lying amongst the rich rank grass luxuriously chewing the cud ; on all sides arose the bleating of sheep ; the fields were dotted with snow-white lambs ; from the farmhouses came the occasional bark of a dog, the quacking of ducks, the clucking of fussy hens escorting their active broods to favourite corners where insects were to be found in plenty ; there was a great peace about the landscape, and standing still in the midst of waving grass and growing corn, Glen, looking to right and left, felt satisfied there was something in all this rich and bounteous country she did not thoroughly understand or appreciate ; but which, if things continued to go well with her, she might learn to value, as wiser and older and cleverer people than herself had done before she was thought of.

She waited for the post at a point where the man made a *détour* ere coming straight on to their cottage, which cottage lay indeed at the extreme limit of his beat.

She expected—what? A letter from Mr. Vassett, or Mr. Pedland, or one of the many editors she had written to, or Mr. Lacere, or perhaps even proof. If once she could see anything of hers in proof, she felt she should take fresh heart, and go on with a braver spirit. Afar off she could hear the rush of one of the early morning trains as it swept through the tranquil valley to London. A collie with whom she was on intimate terms came and licked her hand. The air was full of pleasant sounds and grateful scents, and there was the postman, who, seeing her, paused and took out a letter.

'Only one this morning, miss,' he said; and then, turning down the lane, went to deliver his good and evil tidings to farmhouse and hall and rectory and hovel.

'Only one—from Ned.' Glen sat down on the lowest step of the stile and opened the envelope. As she did this, there came wafted in imagination the familiar sound of the waves—the glitter of the sun upon the sea—the smell of the iodine—the smoke of the kelp fire—the plash of oars—and even the taste of the salt brine upon her lips.

That had been her past—the wild, grand coast—the raving billows—the strip of yellow sand—the frowning headlands—the screaming gulls—the stretching bogs and the treeless expanse of desolate country—and now—— She looked around and smiled half sadly, and drew out Ned's letter.

Ned's letters were of the nature of manuscripts. They were the produce of many hours, in many weeks. They proposed to convey an epitome of the news of the district, and it may at once be said they fulfilled their promise.

There was nothing too great or too little for Ned's pen to exercise itself upon, and Glen's conscience had often reproached her when she remembered how scanty were the tidings she returned in exchange—how closely she kept the secret of what she was doing, hoping, expecting, from this friend of the dear old happy careless days gone by.

As she pulled the enclosure out of the envelope these were the words on which her eyes fell :

'It was mean of you, Glen; I could not have believed it. All the same, though, we wish you success—every one of us. Write soon.—Ned.'

What did this astounding conclusion mean ? She turned the letter over, and found the gist of the whole lay in a postscript hurriedly added, much smeared and blotted, and written evidently in much perturbation of mind. The cat was out of the bag at last. Every soul in Ballyshane, every inhabitant of Artinglass, knew now why Mr. and Miss Westley had gone off in such a hurry to London. Her old admirer, Mr. Dufford, had come down to take the duty at Artinglass while the Rector was ill, and, as chance would have it, he lodged at the Berlin-wool and fancy shop, the owner of which likewise kept the local post-office.

To him came one day a book parcel of manuscript, which, happening to elicit from the postmistress a remark to the effect that 'few of such things came now to Artinglass

since Miss Westley was gone from Ballyshane,'
led to further inquiries, and to a perfect conviction on the part of the whole countryside
that the girl was making her fortune.

Miss Grumley had brought the news to the
Vicarage, believing Glen's old friends would
be only too delighted to hear she was doing so
well. 'They say you are writing for the
Penny Rambler,' added Ned, mentioning a
publication which in those days was relegated
to the kitchen, and deemed too poor and silly
to find favour in the eyes of mothers of families,
'whatever that may be. Miss Grumley has
heard the people who own it pay well. I am
sure I hope they do. But, oh, Glen! why
could you not have told us? mother is quite
hurt. You know if you had been her own
daughter she could not have loved you more.
No wonder your letters were short, and had
nothing in them worth reading. It is only
surprising you could write to us at all, knowing
what you were keeping back;' and then he
added the words previously quoted.

The letter dropped from Glen's fingers.
She had not read, she never did read the first
part of it; she sat for a little while stunned;

she did not feel the sunshine, or hear the birds, or smell the meadowsweet, or see the stretching fields dotted with sheep and lambs. The first thing that roused her attention was the collie licking her hand.

'Oh, Nell!' she exclaimed. 'Oh, Nell, I am miserable!' and laying her cheek on the dog's grizzled head, she cried as if her heart would break.

She was not crying because Ned called her mean and close, though that hurt her sorely, but because her secret had become known to those she wished to keep it from; and all comfort and security and freedom in writing was over.

The very book Mr. Lacere had sold for her could not now be published; it told a story she never would have ventured to have put on paper had she not felt secure under the shelter of the assumed name selected after much thought and mature deliberation. In the work she had introduced her own relations, Lady Emily and others, who seemed to Glen equally objectionable. Her pen had run freely, unrestrained by the slightest fear of consequences while she was writing. It never once occurred to her anyone would ever know who was the author of this remarkable novel ; but now in a moment the whole position was changed, and in despair Glen dried her eyes and tried to consider what she had better do.

Before she reached home her mind was made up. She must get back the manuscript ; no matter what the consequence, that novel must not appear. It was dreadful, it was heart-rending ; but still she could think of no other course. Naturally, Mr. Lacere would be deeply offended ; well, even the forfeiture of his friendship was a result which must be risked. She talked the matter over with her father, who, though more doubtful than his daughter as to the course which ought to be adopted, still did not think it would do to publish the book.

' You had better go to town, Glen,' he said, ' and explain the whole matter to Mr. Lacere. To a certain extent you might be guided by his advice,' added Mr. Westley, who most earnestly desired to shift the burden of this new and sudden responsibility on to the shoulders of some other person.

' I am afraid,' answered Glen, ' there is

nothing to be done, except get back the manuscript. Mr. Lacere will be terribly annoyed. After all his kindness and the trouble he took, too——'

It was mid-day before the girl got into London, and hot, tired, and dusty, reached the welcome shade of the City lanes. To turn into Mr. Lacere's office after the stifling heat of the carriages on the South-Western line, and the glare of the streets that led from the terminus into the heart of the Lord Mayor's kingdom, was like entering some cool grot in the midst of a parched and sandy desert. For a moment she paused in the hall to read the names painted there. Mr. Logan Lacere was the person she wanted, and she wended her way slowly up stairs, thinking as she went how she should begin to say what was in her mind.

She knocked at the panel of the first door she came to, turned the handle, and went in. A gentleman stood behind a desk, and looked across it at her as she walked shyly forward.

He was not her friend ; she had never seen him before, and he seemed perfectly amazed at sight of her.

' Is Mr. Lacere within ?' she asked, feeling as she put the question strangely flurried and uncomfortable.

' *I* am Mr. Lacere,' was the unexpected reply.

Glen stared at the speaker for a moment, and then made this extraordinary statement, ' But you are not *my* Mr. Lacere !'

The stranger smiled. His smile was what most persons would have considered mild, tolerant, reassuring, and benignant, yet in the midst of all her hurry and confusion Glen found time to feel she neither liked it nor him.

She could not have told what the something was which repelled her. She only knew she wished she had not come into the office, and that she was well out of it again and walking back to the station.

Yet the gentleman was well favoured, his manner courteous, and the voice in which he said, ' It is Mr. Logan Lacere you wish to see, I presume ?" gentle and by no means unpleasant.

' Yes,' said Glen ; ' I did not know—that is, I mean——"

Probably it would have been extremely difficult for her to explain what she did mean —at all events she did not try, but stopped at this point.

' He is out at present,' remarked the other Mr. Lacere, coming to her assistance, ' but I do not think it will be long before he returns. If you would like to wait,' and he pulled forward a chair, and with a polite gesture of his hand invited her to be seated.

Glen hesitated—perhaps in all the few years of her life she had never before so hesitated. She glanced round the office, she looked for one swift second in the face of the man who was looking at her : she thought of the hot dusty pavements ; that she was very tired ; that she had no other place to call at unless she turned back to the west and paid Mr. Vassett or Mr. Pedland a visit—for which, perhaps, neither gentleman would be especially grateful ; that she must see Mr. Logan Lacere or else return home with her mission unfulfilled ; that the room was cool and pleasant after the glare of the streets. Nevertheless——

' He is almost certain to be back shortly,' said this strange Mr. Lacere, noticing her hesitation and understanding the cause of it as little as she did.

'If I shall not be intruding——' Glen murmured.

'Not in the least,' was the reply. 'You will have the office to yourself, for I am going out. Should you like to look at the newspaper?' and he handed her the *Times*, which she took mechanically.

There was a clock on the mantelshelf; after Mr. Lacere's departure, it seemed to Glen that she and the timepiece were alone in the world together. She might have been in a far-off desert for any sound of human life which reached her. How silent the whole house seemed—how loud the clock ticked! Glen's heart and the pendulum appeared racing together, but her heart won. Its throbbing distanced the regular beat of the clock, till, growing weary of the conflict, the girl rose, and began pacing the limits of the narrow room. Her life since she came to London had told upon a nervous system never before really put upon its trial; and Glen, who in the days not yet a whole year gone by rode shaggy ponies, and climbed dizzy cliffs, and

walked at the very edge of precipices that looked
sheer down into three hundred fathoms of water,
and stepped without a thought of fear into a
crazy old boat, now found danger in the sudden
stoppage of a train, almost dreaded to cross a
crowded thoroughfare, could not bear the sound
of a clock ticking, and was unable to possess
her soul in patience for half an hour, even
with an office quite to herself, and a whole
copy of the *Times*, advertisement sheet included, for companionship!

Suddenly, as in her restless walk she had
reached a row of bookshelves that lined a
recess opposite the window, and was trying
for the twentieth time to fix her attention
upon the volumes and read their odd-looking
titles, a step sounded on the stairs, and before
she could regain her seat the door of the office
opened, and Mr. Lacere entered.

At sight of the girl, his face, which had previously worn a look of heavy care, lighted up
and brightened instantly.

'Why!' he said, and held out one hand,
while he took off his hat with the other. 'Why!'
and for a moment it seemed as if that were
the only word in the whole of his vocabulary.

' I have come about that book, Mr. Lacere,'
Glen explained. She did not feel afraid now
of his being vexed ; she only felt a great
trouble because of what she had to say.

' You got my letter, I hope ?' This was in-
terrogative.

' Oh yes, and I was so happy and thankful ;
but now that is all over ; it can't be published.'

' Indeed ! why not ? Sit down and tell me
what you mean ;' and thus entreated, Glen re-
sumed her chair, while Mr. Lacere stood leaning against his desk, and with one foot resting
on the rail of an office stool, waited to hear
her explanation.

There was a rest and a strength about the
man, in his voice, his look, his manner, which
soothed Glen's unquiet spirit—as a mother's
cool hand laid on a child's feverish brow seems
to ease the pain in the throbbing temples. At
last the ticking of the clock did not distress
her. Now her heart beat calmly and evenly
as was its wont. Almost before she knew
she had begun her story, it was half told.
Mr. Lacere did not move or speak or interrupt her till she had quite finished. Even

then he remained silent for a moment ere he
said :

'It seems a great pity.'

Pity ! Glen knew more about that than he
did, or at least she thought so ; but she held
her peace while he proceeded:

'It is such an opportunity as may not occur
again for some time.'

'Never,' agreed Glen vehemently ; 'such a
chance is not likely to come to anybody twice
in a lifetime.'

'I would not go quite so far as that,' said
Mr. Lacere, with a smile—oh ! so unlike
the smile of that other Mr. Lacere Glen
felt she mistrusted—'but still, I think you
ought to consider the matter well before you
finally decide on adopting any course.
You must recollect how difficult it is to
get publishers to accept a manuscript at
all.'

Yes, Glen was aware of the fact ; but still
this manuscript must not be printed. She
went over the ground once more, explaining
with greater emphasis than before how dreadful a thing it would be if, now it was known
she wrote, the book were read by any of the

persons who had all unconsciously sat for their portraits in it.

'But why should anyone imagine you to be the author of this particular work ?' asked Mr. Lacere.

Glen thought him dense for putting such a question. She did not say so, but feeling, since Ned's letter, as if she went about with the word AUTHOR branded on her forehead, her manner implied that secrecy now was out of the question ; besides, the work itself bore internal evidence she had produced it.

'People would know,' she declared, 'and besides— Have you read the story, Mr. Lacere ?' she inquired abruptly.

Mr. Lacere confessed he had not—he had glanced at the first page ; but 'I have not much leisure,' he explained, 'and a manuscript is really a formidable affair.'

Glen sighed, but could not controvert a statement which she had heard too often repeated to feel any doubt concerning its accuracy. Experience—even her experience— had taught the truth that a manuscript is the point where humanity draws the line. A man might risk his life for a friend ; but

where, oh! where is the person to be found
who would, unless compelled, plunge into the
depths of inky ' copy' to please or benefit the
nearest and dearest belonging to him ?   Glenarva had still to meet that Curtius upon the
summer's afternoon when she sat in Mr.
Lacere's office, and it may be added she has
not met him yet.

As she remembered how hard she had found
it to get anyone to read through even the
shortest tale, she happened to look up, and
found Mr. Lacere's eyes fixed on her with an
expression which showed he knew of what she
was thinking.

' And as we have got a book accepted,' he
said, as if in amplification of the idea that
had been passing through her mind, ' I do
not want you to lose the advantage gained
without weighing carefully the probable consequences.'

For answer, Glen assured her adviser she
had weighed everything—thought of everything—considered all consequences—and forgotten no possible contingency.

' It is already partly set up,' urged Mr.
Lacere.

The author was willing to pay for any loss that might have been incurred.

'And I had great hopes of being able to get you twenty pounds,' he said, playing the court card he had kept back for the last trick.

Glen drew a long gasping breath—twenty pounds! What a fortune it seemed to reject —then she answered valiantly.

'I must give up even that, Mr. Lacere;' and he understood the case seemed urgent to her, whether it was urgent in reality or not.

Nevertheless, he asked her to think the matter over for a few days, which suggestion the girl negatived, stating, as neither days nor years could make any difference in her sentiments, it would only prolong her misery to defer deciding the affair at once.

'Well, if you think it best,' he remarked, at last, 'I will write to my friend. Yet still——'

Perhaps he was all the more pertinacious in entreating delay, because in his heart he wished she would abandon authorship altogether. He did not feel so sure now as had once been the case that Glen would never make her mark. Some words the reader in that great publishing firm dropped when speaking of the novel impressed him with the idea there might be more in this young person than appeared on the surface.

But she did not look like an author ! Like many another, Mr. Lacere possibly associated authorship in ladies with middle age and spectacles.

That he certainly could have understood, but Glen with her young face and the soft curves of her girlish figure, and her hair which glistened in the sunlight, and her eyes that then held no shadow of the sorrow they were to look on, and her voice with the sound of no tears as yet prisoned in its cadences—was quite another matter.

Here seemed a life to be lived, an existence to be enjoyed, not a battle to be waged or struggle won. Deep within him lay the almost forlorn hope that she would turn back ere it was too late, and abandon a strife he did not believe could conduce to her happiness.

And possibly he was right. It might have been better for Glen and those nearest and dearest to her if she had never written another line.

There are some women for whom even one leaf of the laurel crown proves too heavy a burden, even the faint echo of the world's applause too loud a sound, to whom genius seems but a demon driving its possessor out into dry and stony places, where is no tender grass for the weary feet to tread, and no trickling rills to refresh the tired and parched heart, nay, to whom fame itself becomes a mere mockery to the spirit searching vainly for something it shall never attain on earth.

'Yet still——' that was what he said; but he said no more, for Glen stopped him.

'I must begin all over again, I suppose, but it cannot be helped. I will never write another book founded on fact, so long as I live—never.'

Hearing which statement, Mr. Lacere only looked at the girl more dreamily and speculatively than ever, and hoped with silent earnestness she might never write another book at all.

'I am ashamed,' said Glen, rising, 'to have taken up so much of your time.'

As she spoke she glanced at the clock, and felt really shocked to see how long the inter-

view had lasted ; and then she added some
words about feeling grateful for all his kindness, which indeed she found hard to utter,
not because her heart was empty, but because
it was at that moment too full.

He did not answer directly; he only observed, a little coldly as it seemed to Glen, he
wished he could have been of more use ; and
she was going to take her leave, with the consciousness of feeling rebuffed and chilled, when
he said he meant to see her to the station.

'Oh, I could not think of giving you so
much trouble !' exclaimed Glen.

'And I could not think of allowing you to
walk back there alone,' he declared decisively.

So through the long, busy streets, where the
westering sun was streaming, they paced slowly
side by side.   It was a happy walk for one of
them—perhaps the happiest walk he ever had
in all his life.   On his arm rested the hand he
would have liked to take and hold for ever in
his own ; the voice he had learned to love
best in all the world murmured in his ear; the
glamour he had escaped hitherto held him
captive then.   It was an enchanted river that
glided away that evening beneath the bridges

to the far away ocean he could not see. Vane and dome and pinnacle were lit with the glory which streams upon every earthly landscape but once in a human life, and then—then it was all over, and she did not know that he had been walking through a Paradise, the gates of which closed behind him as the train glided out of the station.

No, she did not know; and he strode back along streets whence sunshine seemed to have departed, to his office, where he worked hard and late, perhaps to finish some allotted task, perhaps to drown thought.

. A man Hope had ever hitherto kept even step with in his darkest hours, but who for once heard only the rustle of her trailing garments, as slowly and reluctantly the angel that had upheld him in the worst troubles he was ever yet called upon to encounter left him at this crisis alone, and with uplifted hands covering the radiance of her face departed through the night, which was but little blacker than his worldly prospects.

CHAPTER IX.

YES.

A YEAR had come and gone since that October morning when the Irish steamer entered Morecambe Bay. The summer, which always, no matter how long and how fine it may be, seems so short a space, was over. London was looking its worst and dullest in damp autumnal weather, and Mr. Westley and his daughter were back in town, having decided their country cottage was too far from everywhere, and that the great literary battle could only be properly fought out within the metropolitan bills of mortality.

It was a wretched season—worse, far worse, Glen decided, than that which inaugurated her search for a publisher. A green winter,

which always and ever makes such fat church-
yards; dull, damp, warm, depressing; terribly
trying to a girl accustomed to Atlantic breezes,
to pure mountain air, to a climate which,
though often mild through the worst months
of the year, was never enervating.

The weather, however, in London, or the
medicine he was taking, seemed to suit Mr.
Westley better than the lonely moors in Middlesex, the glorious summer sunshine, the
simple remedies he had before experimented
with. Apparently the course of his malady
was stayed; those cruel ' chills ' ceased to shake
his frame; his appetite, which had in the
country rebelled against the simple food they
were there at least able to obtain fresh and
pure, accepted in town anything provided for
it. So far as her father was concerned, Glen
felt happier; but her own prospects were far
from bright.

' I am going back,' she thought—' back—
back—back.'

In the lives of most authors there occurs, I
imagine, a crisis when they stop disgusted, or
else go on in sheer despair. They either turn
to something else, or otherwise persevere not

from any real hope they feel of ultimate success, but because they know they must 'see
the thing out.'

Such a crisis had come to Glenarva Westley.
If at that juncture she could have seen her way
to adding twenty or five-and-twenty pounds a
year to their income, she would have put the
cover on her ink-bottle, laid her pen in the
stand, and said, 'Well, I have tried that, and
it has failed. I was mistaken in thinking I
could write.'

As matters stood, she did rack her brain
considering whether she could not make
money by any means; but, alas! save for
needlework the girl seemed then to have no gift.

She was fairly educated, but she did not
know enough to teach; and if she had, would
rather have swept a crossing. She played well,
but was nothing of a musician; her drawing
was of the usual commonplace character; for
languages she had no more aptitude than for
arithmetic. No one could have affirmed with
truth that Glenarva Westley was a dunce,
yet in most branches of learning a school-
mistress would have said she was 'singularly
backward.' She had not even a speaking ac-

quaintance with any 'ology. Such gifts as she possessed—and they were not many—did not lie in the direction of money-making.

'I am fit for nothing,' she thought one night in a frenzy of self-depreciation, and sobbed herself to sleep.

Things were not going well with her. The novel Mr. Pedland published turned out, so far as she was concerned, a hopeless failure. The papers had not a good word to say for it; the critics were beautifully unanimous in making merry over her finest passages—in exposing the absurdity of her plot, the faults in her grammar, the solecisms of which she was guilty, the meagreness of her ideas, the poverty of her invention, the tallness of her talk, and the impossibility of many things which were literal facts ever having happened.

The very fierceness of the attack caused Glen to gird on her armour. She was disappointed, but not beaten; disheartened, but not driven back.

The non-success of 'Tyrrel's Son, by G. B. W. Shane,' did not send her crying to bed; it was the weary, weary waiting of the days and weeks and months which came after.

Though even 'Tyrrel's Son' held a cruel and terrible disappointment for the girl—the particulars of which it may not be totally unprofitable to summarize here for the benefit of those young authors who think the way to fame lies along a well-turfed alley bordered with flowers and shaded by trees, in which the nightingale jug-jugs ceaselessly.

Amongst many other things not so nice as herself, Mrs. Beattie possessed a maiden aunt who, having as great a craze for travel as Madame Pfeiffer, spent all her small fortune in marching from pillar to post, from city to city, and from land to land.

As good or evil fortune would have it, just about the time Glen's novel was published, this lady arrived in London from some twentieth-rate Spa in Germany; whither she had repaired to test the virtues of the waters and the merits of a certain local physician concerning an 'affection of the ear' she had contracted while residing, for economy's sake, in uncomfortable lodgings where she was obliged to sleep exposed to the draughts from window, chimney, and door.

Her first act was to look up the Westleys—

her next to merge her very identity in Glen's novel.

Knocking about the world as she had done, it was her fortune to have come in contact with all sorts and conditions of authors—except good. She had met and discoursed with Miss This and Mrs. That and Mr. The Other, who each and all vied in telling 'travellers' tales' concerning that land, the mysteries of which can never be fully known, save to those who have carried the burden and passed through the trouble, and felt the heat and the cold of the long, long years filled with disappointment, and trial, and success.

All enthusiasm, she carried off Miss Glen's first venture. She read it—she approved. She said the girl had a 'great future' before her. She wrote that by the most curious coincidence she had formed an acquaintance in her then lodgings with a gentleman who could, she found, influence the young author's future most materially.

'He is on the *Times*,' she explained. 'He can get you a review. The moment you receive this letter, send me another copy of "Tyrrel's Son," or, if you have not one, go to

your publisher and procure the novel without
delay. If Mr. Elphin has it at once he will
put you a good notice in the *Times*, which
ought to be worth ever so much money to
you.'

On the strength of this letter Glen repaired
to Mr. Pedland, who smiled and said he had
heard so much of ' that sort of thing' he did
not attach the slightest importance to it ;
which observation rather nettled Miss Westley,
for, as she told him, her friend would not have
promised her a review unless she felt certain of
being able to get it.

Word led to word, and answer to answer,
till at length Mr. Pedland ' backed his opinion,'
as the lower orders are so fond of phrasing the
matter, with a memorandum to the effect that
if a review of ' Tyrrel's Son' appeared in the
Times—not as an advertisement (those were the
days when advertisements in extremely small
type, and the charge for which was very high,
were inserted in the body of the paper)—within a month, he would give her seventy pounds.

Placing this document, about which she had
happily sufficient common-sense to keep silence
during the impending interview, securely in

her pocket, Glen, with the three volumes filled by the doings of 'Tyrrel's Son,' and other people, tied up in a neat brown-paper parcel, wended her way to Miss Stanuel's lodgings, where that lady, who if not saving was nothing, received her in a dingy bedchamber, having only, as she explained, the occasional use of a sitting-room for which she did not pay.

'It is fortunate,' she exclaimed, 'that you happened to come at this particular time, for Mr. Elphin has not gone out yet. I will introduce you to him; and mind, you must be on your best and prettiest behaviour, for he is a person who can either make or mar you.' Having finished which sentence, so admirably calculated to set the young author at her ease and render her manners natural and pleasing, Miss Stanuel left her visitor alone for a moment, while she herself went and apprised the great man of the impending interview.

Glen had already passed through some curious experiences, and seen some strange sights in the course of her London life; but she certainly considered this 'power on the *Times*' not the least singular person who had come across her path.

He was a short, dark, dirty-looking individual, who rose and bowed as she entered,
and then sat down again beside a table
strewed with papers. He had been writing,
and, for greater convenience, doing it with coat
sleeves pulled up, and wristbands—not over-
clean—turned back. He did not look as if he
had washed himself for a long time, or as if
the *Times* paid handsomely for the work he
did. His manner was curt, not to say rude,
but Miss Stanuel followed his utterances with
the rapt and earnest gaze of admiring belief.

'Are you paying attention, young lady?' she
would say to Glen, after the delivery of some
truism as old and hackneyed as that water
finds its level. 'Now, don't forget this—be
sure you remember every word Mr. Elphin
speaks. It is not often it falls to the lot of beginners, more especially to a chit like you, to
get advice from the fountain-head.' To an
outsider the whole affair would have seemed
inexpressibly ludicrous. The brazen self-
assurance of the gentleman without whom the
Times must have sunk into oblivion; Glen's
amazed contemplation of the celebrated writer;
and Miss Stanuel's almost worshipping regard,

composed a spectacle which indeed it seemed
a pity should have been so entirely destitute of
an audience. Afterwards Glen felt too much
provoked to laugh about the matter. It was
the first time she had been made a fool of,
though it may here be remarked it was not the
last.

'Now, shall I cut this book for you?' suggested Miss Stanuel, when the distinguished
writer seemed inclined to intimate that the
interview had lasted quite long enough.

'No, thank you,' said Mr. Elphin loftily;
'I always like to cut for myself as I go on.'

Miss Stanuel looked triumphantly at Glen
as he made this statement.

'Well, we will not take up any more of your
valuable time,' she remarked.

'I am going out,' he answered—as one who
should say, 'I'll take very good care you
don't.'

'And I am sure Miss Westley can never feel
sufficiently grateful to you.'

'Oh! that's nothing,' exclaimed Mr. Elphin,
but whether his words referred to Miss Westley's gratitude or his own good offices it was
difficult to conjecture.

The days went by—the weeks—a month—
and still no review appeared; instead there
came a note from Miss Stanuel, saying she felt
dreadfully angry with Glen.

'Mr. Elphin tells me "Tyrrel's Son" is *very
poor indeed*, that you could not have taken
any pains with it, and that you never will succeed unless you produce something a great deal
better than that. Of course, even in your own
interests, it was impossible for him to insert a
review of such a book. He assures me he has
done the very kindest thing possible in taking
no notice whatever of it.'

'I am not surprised,' observed Mr. Pedland,
when Glen repeated some of these encouraging
remarks to him. 'I have seen and heard too
much of that sort of thing to believe it. If
your friend had been as good as his word, I
should have felt very much surprised indeed.'

Had the author of 'Tyrrel's Son' thought
of telling Mr. Pedland of Miss Stanuel's
obliging offer to cut the pages, and Mr. Elphin's
refusal, he could have formed a shrewd conjecture as to what the gentleman on the *Times*
had done with her book, and how he spent the
few shillings he got for it!

This was all bad and disappointing, but it did not seem to Glen so bad and utterly disheartening as the fact that when Mr. Lacere took her latest manuscript to the great publishing house from which she felt obliged to withdraw her former book, it was 'declined with thanks,' the reader telling him afterwards he did not consider it nearly so good as the first.

Mr. Vassett also made no sign of entertaining any mad desire to secure a book by the 'gifted young author.' He was very kind and very friendly, but he did not seem to 'see his way' any more clearly than had been the case the first day he saw her. Glen felt that 'getting into print,' on which she had so pinned her faith, was a mere mockery and delusion—more particularly after one of the partners in a very well-known firm told her kindly she had better for the future not mention the fact of Mr. Pedland having published anything of hers.

' His works do not stand well,' explained this gentleman ; 'they are regarded in the same light as the "Minerva Press" novels were formerly.'

Mr. Vassett laughed when Glen told him

this. She went to him for comfort, but he
could not deny the soft impeachment brought
against poor Mr. Pedland.

'I dare say he does a business which he
makes satisfactory to himself,' he said ; 'but
he has not brought out anything remarkable.'

'Except in the way of badness, I am told,'
added Glen. 'I hear if his name is on a book
it is at once stamped as feeble, poor, and
trashy.'

'Well,' answered Mr. Vassett, 'he has not
the monopoly of dull novels ; the fact is, there
are very few written worth publishing at all.'

'I wonder—I wonder,' cried Glen, 'if ever
I shall write anything worth publishing.'

She would have felt immensely obliged to
Mr. Vassett had he replied he was certain of it ;
but he made no reply of the kind.

He only hazarded a vague statement to the
effect that out of all the authors he had known,
scarcely one had achieved what he should call
a great success ; but at the same time he implied he thought it not totally impossible that
after a few years, when his visitor had seen
more, and thought more, and read more, she

might be able to produce a book he would feel justified in considering.

Meantime, however, as Glen had no intention of waiting a moment longer than she could help, she went occasionally to one or other of the new publishers, who then, as now, were constantly springing up like mushrooms.

If they did not determine, however, to have nothing to do with Miss Westley within the first five minutes, they were sure to want a portion of the expenses paid, or a certain number of subscribers guaranteed, or a known name on the title-page as editor.

It was weary work, more especially as Glen often took a most intense dislike to some of these gentry. She said something about this one day to Mr. Vassett when Mr. Pierson was present, and the latter made a laughing remark, to the effect that her instinctive aversions seemed to be wonderfully accurate.

'Why do you dislike Mr. Blank so much?' he asked.

'I am sure I can't tell,' answered Glen; 'I always either like or do not like people at once.'

'And do you never find occasion to change

your opinion, Miss Westley?' asked Mr. Vassett.

'I have not yet,' she said.

'Instinct,' suggested Mr. Pierson.

'I suppose,' observed Mr. Vassett didactically, 'that Providence, having denied women reason, gives them instinct as a compensation.' And then they all laughed, and Glen declared she thought a little reason had been given to her, and Mr. Vassett answered, 'No, it had not; why should she be an exception to the rest of her sex?'

'You trust to your instinct,' he advised; 'that won't deceive you.'

There came a time in Glenarva's life when in anguish and bitterness she remembered those lightly spoken words, when she understood from sad experience a woman's best reason is but a will-o'-the-wisp, leading her on over marsh and brake and quagmire; while one swift intuition will, if followed in dumb, unquestioning faith, take her safely to the end of whatever road—darksome or light—she may be travelling.

During all that period of doubt and gloom, the Westleys were cheered on their way by the

kindly advice and the staunch friendship of
Glen's Mr. Lacere. Like Glen herself, he had
his troubles, which assumed the prosaic form
of pecuniary losses. He talked a good deal to
Mr. Westley on the subject of his own reverses
and disappointments, and for so reserved a
man was extraordinarily frank in stating the
extent to which he found himself embarrassed.
Mr. Westley, who had forgotten the few days
of his own experience during which he was not
harassed, listened to these revelations with
sympathy, but without alarm. Mr. Lacere had
a business of some sort—a profitable business;
he would soon be able to make more money.
Anyone almost ought to be able to make
money in London. What opportunities there
were in the modern Babylon; what riches,
what marvellous chances—ah! if he had come
to London when first he left Glenarva, they
would never have been poor. He was strong
then, comparatively, and younger, and more
active; but now he lay back in his chair and
thought of his wasted life, and the hill he was
descending, and listened while Mr. Lacere
talked about his own prospects, and trials, and
hopes; and what he trusted to do, and what

he expected to achieve, with the small amount
of attention he was able to spare from the contemplation of his personal affairs. Mr. Westley
marvelled a little at these confidences till one
evening, when a glimmer of the state of the
case dawned upon his mind.

He shrank back involuntarily from the light,
and closed his eyes against it; but when he
looked again the light was still there, growing
clearer and clearer as he gazed.

Mr. Lacere was in love with Glen—his Glen
—he did not feel a doubt on the subject; he
could not be mistaken. He would ask him for
her; and when this request came, what answer
should be given?

For hours that night he lay wide awake
thinking, considering, doubting, deciding.
Glen, his motherless daughter; Glen, who
would be left all alone in the world if, or
rather when, Death should call for him, and
say, 'Now I want you; come;' Glen, who on
the face of the wide earth did not possess a
relation for whom she cared or that would be
likely to care for her; Glen, who would have
little or no money; Glen, who could never, he
felt, return to the old life she had, drowned in

tears, left that October day which seemed to her so far back in the mystic past; Glen, who had never been, so far as he knew, in love with anybody, and to whom he believed it would be a terrible surprise and shock to find that Mr. Lacere was in love with her.

'*She* must decide,' thought Mr. Westley ere he fell into a troubled sleep, from which he awoke with a start and that sense of impending trouble which it is so hard to exorcise. And 'Glen must decide for herself' was the answer he gave Mr. Lacere when that gentleman asked if he would trust the girl's happiness to him.

With the memory of Mr. Dufford's rejection in his recollection, Mr. Westley felt doubtful as to what Glen might say, and his manner indicated this doubt so strongly that Mr. Lacere would have deferred the evil hour had Glen's father not remarked :

'If she says " Yes," I shall not make any objection. I wish, of course, your means had been better; but money, though much, is not everything, and I believe you would try to make her happy.'

Glen did not, however, say 'Yes'—she said

' No'—not as she had spoken the word to Mr. Dufford, but rather after the manner of one on whom the proposal came too suddenly, and who did not exactly know her own mind. 'She had not thought about marriage.' 'She was not disposed to marry anyone.' 'She was very sorry—she liked Mr. Lacere very much—she liked him better than anyone she had ever seen, except her father and the boys.' No ; she liked him ' better than the boys, because he was older and wiser,' and knew 'more about everything.' 'Still, she could not marry him.' She 'hoped they would remain good friends.' 'It would grieve her greatly if he ceased to come and talk with her papa,' and she felt ' very grateful,' and ' truly grieved ;' and Mr. Lacere, who was not a bold wooer, and had not frittered away his affections on a dozen pretty women, quitted the house a good deal disheartened, and Glen went to her own room and had a little cry, after which she sat gravely and quietly down to needlework, and did not speak till Mr. Westley broke the ice, and asked her plainly what answer she had given a very honest gentleman.

Then Glen told him her mind so far as she

knew it herself, and Mr. Westley saw clearly enough that there stood in Mr. Lacere's way no real obstacle.

Glen had her own notions about love and lovers, gathered from hearsay, gleaned from books, evolved, perhaps, out of her internal consciousness; and it is only fair to say that neither Mr. Lacere's love-making nor Mr. Lacere himself realized even the poorest of her ideals on the subject. For one thing, the affair was to her feeling all far too serious and commonplace. The glamour of wooing should preface a proposal. She wished she could have known what was in his heart during those long walks and talks which took place among the Middlesex moors.

Vaguely she understood she had lost something that could never be given to her again. She was not old enough, or wise enough, though she had written books, and thought the whole experience of life was plain reading before her eyes, to put in words to herself the truth that the lover should always precede the possible husband, that the two characters should not come suddenly on the stage of a girl's life together; the prosaicism of marriage, the thought of ways and means, the fifty practical considerations which must obtrude themselves when the whole future of existence is concerned, are matters that ought to be led up to gradually—wandered into through fanciful alleys carpeted with moss, bordered with flowers, arched over with roses, within sight and sound of sparkling fountains—alleys where it is always summer, where the birds never cease singing, and to which, amid the thousand sordid cares and petty troubles of dull wedded experience, memory can revert as to a bright holiday—so bright, so beautiful, that even the bare recollection of its sunshine, its birds, its songs, can light up the whole of the dull after-days of existence with gleams of that golden glory.

Years afterwards Glen knew this was what she had missed, but it took years and years and years for her to understand it was the accursed money-troubles which dogged every step of his way—that tied the man's tongue, and froze the words trembling on his lips, and kept him silent when speech had been the truest wisdom, and made him, when he did make up his mind, taking his future in his

hand, to ask her to share it, receive her doubtful ' No ' almost as a final answer, and say to
his own soul, ' It is best so. What right have
I, with my poor fortunes, to "expect" any
woman to marry me ?'

And yet—he did not know ; he could not
receive his rejection as absolute ; he would try
again, and, if her answer was still the same,
never see her more. There were other places
on earth besides London. He would go
abroad.

He had thought of leaving England when he
sustained the loss that had during the course
of the previous summer thrown him so far
back in the world, and now he decided, that
in case Glen refused him a second time, he
would bid her and all his friends good-bye,
and try whether in another country fate might
hold a better fortune for him than had been
the case hitherto.

But when he repeated his question Glen
did not say ' No.' She had thought the
matter out by herself. She talked a little to
her father.

' My dear,' said Mr. Westley, ' you have
drawn many a hero after your own pattern

out of your own fancy ; but you will never, so long as you live, meet with a better man or truer gentleman than Mr. Lacere.'

'I believe that, papa,' she answered, and yet still she hesitated.

She did not tell her father why—perhaps she could not have told herself. Some of those heroes of romance were, it might be, stopping the way, or, as is more than probable, Glen felt there were greater practical objections in the way of marrying Mr. Lacere than Mr. Westley seemed to realize.

One thing, however, was quite certain—she must now either say 'Yes,' or 'No,' without any future possibility of reconsidering her decision. When this calm, quiet, earnest suitor came for the second time, she understood he would not ask her again if she refused him. They would part, and part for ever. Could she let him go ? She felt it would be impossible. Very patiently—far too patiently to accord with any romantic ideas— he waited for her answer. Glen looked about the room, at the worn carpet, at the old-fashioned chairs, the pembroke table, the glass over the mantelpiece—everywhere, anywhere save at those wistful brown eyes, at the yearning expression on that grave, worn face.

'Will you not speak?' he said at last. 'Tell me, if you can, the best—or—the—worst.'

Then she did look at him with the anxious, questioning look a child's face wears when it trustfully turns to its mother for a solution of all perplexing doubts and difficulties.

'I don't want to say "Yes," and I don't want to say "No,"' she explained.

His heart gave a wild leap, but he asked quietly, '*Can't* you say "Yes"?'

'Yes, then,' she answered. The words were spoken almost in a whisper, yet they sounded to his ears like the crash of joy-bells smiting the stillness of a summer's noon.

'Oh, my darling!' and for a moment she felt frightened at the vehemence of his tone; the revulsion of feeling—the knowledge that doubt was ended and security begun was almost more than he could bear; then: 'May God do so to me, and more, if ever I give you cause to repent your consent!'

It was but a young thing—a young, slight

thing, though possessed of a grand courage
and a big soul—he gathered to his heart and
kissed as he had never kissed woman born of
woman before.

If she had known, if she had only known
that in the whole of his life she was the first
creature he felt he could take in his arms and
call wholly his own—something to care for;
something to live for; something to work for;
something to die for !

Is it well or ill, I wonder, that we, each
and all of us, have so little real comprehension
of past, present, and future ?   Well, possibly
—or we should for ever in our uncertainty
stand shivering on the brink of life's wide
tideless river.   As for Glen, just as she was
wont at Ballyshane to step into the old crazy
boat that generally scudded to its destination
with one gunwale under water—so she now
tripped into her place in the barque which
was to convey her across life's heaviest seas.
Whilst, as regards Mr. Lacere, he had but the
faintest notion of the sort of passenger he was
taking on board.

He loved her—that was enough for him.
He did not think then or afterwards how

perilous an experiment it is for experience to undertake the guidance of ignorance; for Middle Age to say, 'I will pilot Youth, and Enthusiasm, and Impatience, and Hope "to the harbour where it would be."'

CHAPTER X.

SUCCESS.

OR once father and lover were of the same mind. Mr. Lacere wished for a speedy marriage. Mr. Westley raised no objection. He did not see the good, he said, of long engagements. 'After a short time,' he added, 'when I have got accustomed to the idea of Glen being your wife, as well as my daughter, I will give her to you with a feeling of perfect reliance.' And so it came to be understood that during the course of the autumn Miss Westley was to be transformed into Mrs. Lacere.

So far, diplomatic arrangements between the two families had been friendly. Their limited

intercourse partook of the nature of state
visits. Mr. Westley, always somewhat of a
recluse, showed, Glen could not but observe,
even less than his usual disposition to cultivate
close and intimate social relations with the
members comprising Mr. Lacere's household.
He said little about them, and the little he
did say was in their praise ; but Glen knew
perfectly well her father did not take to the
ladies of the Lacere family, and that, as if, by
common consent, the fact of their existence
was usually ignored.

' I hope, Glen,' he remarked on one occasion,
' you will always be good friends with your
husband's family.'

' I hope so too,' answered Glen, stitching at
a piece of work she held in her hand. When
not writing she was generally sewing.

' He has no idea of our living with them, I
trust ?'

' Good gracious, no, papa !'

' Because, dear, I should not like to give
you up altogether; and I do not think—indeed I am sure it would not be desirable for
what one may describe as three families to
reside under one roof.'

'You may be very sure, papa, I am going to live with you, and not with Miss Humphries.'

Now Miss Humphries was the name of the lady who was supposed to preside over the domestic arrangements at Kentish Town, where the Laceres resided, and Glen managed to impart such an amount of decision into the manner of her reply that Mr. Westley paused and looked at her for a moment in doubt before he made any further observation. He had often before wondered whether it would not be wise for him to draw out some charts for his daughter's future guidance through the Lacere country, as, for instance, 'I should not be too intimate with them, Glen;' 'It is always competent to increase the amount of intimacy, but ungracious to lessen it;' 'Their ideas may not be yours, still, that is no reason why you and they should not remain excellent friends.' But he never expressed one of these axioms in words, and now all he said was :

'So long as that is clearly understood, my dear——'

'Oh, there shan't be any misconception on that point !' Glen assured him ; and once again

Mr. Westley took refuge in silence, feeling that, while he could not define where it was, a hitch had arisen in some place, and that, although no one gave open expression to the fact, things were not going quite so smoothly as they ought.

He entertained no doubt matters would right themselves after a little time. Meanwhile he and Glen seemed tacitly to have arrived at the conclusion that ' least said,' even between themselves, ' would be the soonest mended.'

The consciousness that his daughter had not a sixpence to her fortune, that she was indeed a beggar maid, tied his tongue. A not unnatural reticence about expressing her sentiments concerning the family she was about to enter kept Glenarva herself silent, whilst Mr. Lacere, who would only have felt too thankful had anyone planned his future course for him, held his peace, because, although he was aware the Westleys were poor, he did not in the least know how modest and moderate were the expectations of both father and child ; that they would have been perfectly content to set up house on the most

humble scale, and confine the domestic expen-
diture to a point far below any on which he
had hitherto supposed respectable establish-
ments could be kept going.

As for Glen herself, her first introduction to
the ladies of Mr. Lacere's family had proved a
most bitter disappointment. She was privileged to make their acquaintance before any
question arose of lovers and marriage, and she
brought accordingly a perfectly unprejudiced
mind to bear upon the subject. With that
fatal desire to bespeak a favourable judgment
which generally impresses the hearer falsely,
Mr. Lacere had spoken in such terms of his
womenkind as had led Glen to believe they
must indeed be little, if at all, lower than the
angels. They were possessed of every possible
virtue. They were unselfish, devoted, amiable,
clever, industrious, forbearing, charitable in
word and deed, thoughtful for others and
forgetful of themselves. Like Lady O'Loony,
in a word, they were 'bland, passionate,
religious.' One of them painted in water-
colours with delicacy, fancy, and skill; another
understood everything in music there was
to understand ; while a third was a poetess of

no mean order ; and Miss Humphries posed alternately as a house brownie and an excellent cook, a sick nurse without compeer, and a manager such as is not often met in this wasteful, ill-regulated world.

Unhappily for herself, instead of following Charles Lamb's admirable example, Glen idealized all the persons thus presented for her admiration. Mr. Lacere believed he was giving her merely rough outlines of forms he had from childhood been accustomed to admire, and the girl set herself at work to finish each portrait off with a delicacy the lady who painted miniatures most exquisitely on ivory might have tried to emulate in vain.

If they had been saints, and heroines, and martyrs, they could not have realized her fancy sketch, and as they were nothing of the sort, the disappointment she experienced proved proportionately severe.

Poor Glen ! with all the will in the world she could not rush into friendship with any one of the four. She was quite content to believe they were most admirable people— possessed of every quality with which she had heard them credited, but at the same time she felt very sure—she never felt more sure of anything—she never could have much to do with them ; that her way and their way lay in quite opposite directions, and that while Mr. Lacere seemed everything that was pleasant, she could not really like any one of the ladies, who, according to his account, had a monopoly of earthly virtues.

And if this were the case before she was engaged, it grew to be ten times more the case afterwards.

All in vain the Misses Lacere embraced and welcomed her 'as a sister.' In vain Miss Humphries said, ' Now you will have *all* of us to love you, darling !' In vain they repeated singly and in chorus that ' though they had never thought a wife could be found good enough for the best man that ever lived, they were more than satisfied with his choice.'

Glen could not get up any enthusiasm on her own side. She could not adopt as sisters women old enough to be her mother, but who were far more gushing than she had ever been even at five years of age. She could not say she loved one of them, for she did not. She failed to feel that the fact of meeting with their approval filled her with the delight and astonishment it perhaps ought to have done; and lastly, there is little doubt that even then she believed in her heart every word they spoke lacked the ring of truth.

When a man has kept unmarried till middle life, his womankind must indeed be more than human to look upon the designing person who has ensnared him with approval, more especially when that person presents herself in the guise of a ' chit of a girl,' a ' tocherless lass,' a stranger, an author, and, worse than all, a native of Ireland.

The Misses Lacere were narrow-minded, prejudiced, selfish. They had lived in themselves and among themselves, till they lost all knowledge, if they ever possessed any, of a world outside their own petty aims, hopes, fears, interests. Instead of being glad the man was at last going to try to make a little happiness for himself in life, they were heartily sorry. They talked the matter over with bated breath, with solemn shakes of the head, with many ' Ahs !' and ' Yes, indeeds !' and ' We never thoughts,' and ' It is to be hoped it will turn out better than we expects ;' and all the time Mr. Lacere believed they were perfectly sincere in their praise of Glen ; and Glen, though she felt they did not like her, and knew she did not like them, hoped she would outgrow her prejudices in time, and that, after all, if Mr. Lacere was pleased and satisfied, and her father felt content and happy, it did not much matter what anybody else thought on the subject.

Mr. Lacere and the Misses Lacere and Miss Humphries were especially careful at a very early period of the engagement to tell Glen the exact state of their pecuniary relations.

The ladies of the family were utterly without fortune.

' Well, so am I,' said Glen, which fact, if she could only have realized the truth, did not tend to render the position easier.

She was only laudably anxious to make her relations who were to be, feel that as she was in precisely the same condition as themselves, they need not be uncomfortable about their own impecuniosity.

The wisdom of adding ' another pauper to the domestic difficulty,' to quote the Mr. Lacere who was not hers, might be questionable ; but this view of things had not then

occurred to Glenarva Westley. She did not
come of a stock remarkable for worldly
prudence. The drain thus indicated upon a
man's income failed to strike even Mr.
Westley with dismay. He regarded it as he
might a jointure, a settlement, or a mortgage
on an estate ; that it was optional with Mr.
Lacere to continue or discontinue it, was an
idea which failed to strike either father or
daughter. Neither was made of the material
which would take from another what he had.
None of the Laceres need have felt any uneasi-
ness on that score. Poor though they were,
the Westleys had not, to quote an Irish
phrase, ' a mean drop of blood in their
bodies.'

No fear of the young wife in this case
coming in and sweeping the decks clean for
her own benefit, her father aiding and abet-
ting. Glen was prepared to do with limited
means married, as she had done with limited
means single ; only she would have preferred
to make the trial without the gushing
endearments of her future relations. Words
cannot express the disfavour with which Glen
beheld middle-aged women comporting them-

selves as if in their first teens ; heard her
future husband called, ' Mordy, my treasure !'
or, 'My precious Mordy !' or, ' Mordy,
dearest darling !' when not addressed by
some ridiculous pet name, which it is not too
much to say made the girl—who was somewhat disposed to exalt her future husband
into a hero, and worship him accordingly—
shiver.

It was over this matter Glen became
possessed of a curious involvement of family
history.

Said Mr. Lacere :

' I have never yet, dear, heard you speak
my Christian name ;' and he looked at her a
little anxiously.

Glen fidgeted with the object nearest her
ere she answered :

' Your first name is long, and I do not like
to hear it shortened. May I call you by your
second—Logan ? I think that is so beautiful ?'

' It is a surname, Glen,' he explained ; 'my
father's people were Logans, till one of them
intermarried with a Miss Lacere, an heiress.
He took her name and got her money, and
that was the beginning of all our misfortunes.'

Glen thought this over at great length, and took an early opportunity of referring the question to Miss Lacere.

'You don't sign yourself Logan-Lacere?' she suggested.

'Oh dear no! *we* are not Logan-Laceres, I am happy to say—*we* have nothing to do with the Logans.'

'How does that happen?' asked Glen, mystified.

'Don't you know? Why, when Mordy's father died, after a time his mother married our dear papa, Owen Lacere.'

'But you are older than he is,' interrupted Glen, thoroughly mystified.

'Of course we are; we had lost our darling mamma three years when papa married again.'

'Wait a moment, wait a moment,' entreated Glen; 'then what relation are you to—to— Logan?'

'What do you mean? We are his sisters, of course.'

'That's impossible,' said Glen, with an energy which proved how exceedingly anxious she was to sever the Logan-Lacere connection.

'My dear, we have been always just the

same in love as though we were the closest blood relations. Poor papa always said, " Whatever you do, never forsake Mordy;" and we haven't. We have from the first felt the same to him as if he had been our own, own brother, and I am sure when darling Claudine died, if she had been aunt's very own niece she couldn't have fretted more about her.'

' I am getting lost,' observed Glen. ' Where does Claudine come ?'

' Claudine was dear Philip's wife.'

' I give it up,' cried the future Mrs. Logan-Lacere. ' I can't follow the matter at all.'

' And yet it is as simple as A B C. Our dear papa was Owen Lacere, who married for his second wife the widow of Logan-Lacere— the father of our precious Mordy and his sister Claudine. Claudine married our darling papa's nephew, and so——'

' You are not one of you a drop's blood, as we say in Ireland, to Logan ?'

' If you like to put it that way, of course ;' and Miss Lacere drew herself up offended. ' Though as for what you call a " drop's blood," we were all cousins, and we all love one

another, oh, so dearly ! and this question of
relationship never was raised till——'

'Till somebody cared to raise it, I suppose,'
said Glen wearily.

She thought during those days she should
have lost her senses. What with trying to
unravel the mystery of the Lacere connection ;
with holding her tongue concerning them to
her father ; with practising reticence about his
relations to a man she felt she could not bear
to wound ; with her own non-success ; with
something about her father she could not
understand ; and with an attack of neuralgia
which for months never left her, which drove
her out of bed at four o'clock in the morning,
and kept her pacing her room till after twelve
at night ; which seemed as if, like a dog, it took
her in its teeth and worried her ; which starved
her almost, because the moment a meal was
spread the inexorable pain came to table also
and prevented her eating. She went and had
a tooth out, and as she returned from the
doctor's, met with that dreadful sympathy
which was the curse of her new life.

'That poor little girl has got the face-ache,'
said one City 'swell' to another as she passed

the pair, holding a handkerchief to her mouth, suffering literally agonies.

Yet upon the whole, if she could have known it, both the City and the West-End swell was very good to her in those days, very good indeed. He troubled her a little, as was only to be expected considering how fresh she was from the wild seashore, and the solitary moor, and the lonely hillside; but he certainly did, upon the whole, respect her ignorance and her innocence, and left her as free to traverse the London streets as though her unaccustomed feet were traversing some lonely path in the domain which might still have been her father's, had she never been.

That awful pain—that maddening, racking pain, which through the whole of the long summer never completely left Glen an hour's physical ease, rendered her almost indifferent to the shortcomings of the Lacere family, and blinded her—oh, poor Glen!—to a mysterious change in her father.

Other people saw he was getting to look very old and frail; but Glen though it was only the hot weather that tried him, and went out on wonderful quests after new-laid eggs and milk fresh from the cow, the only procurable luxuries that his fitful appetite affected.

'My darling, when are we to be married?' asked Mr. Lacere, in the beginning of that brilliant August.

'Oh! any time,' she answered indifferently. 'Next month, if papa and I are both better.'

'Both better,' he thought. 'Oh, Glen—my Glen!'

The first hint of the tempest came shortly after. Glen and her father had been out together, and as, on their return, he went up the stairs, he staggered, and would have fallen but for her swift protecting hand.

'I think I have over-tired myself,' he said; and still Glen looked forward to a future when, in the pretty house at Sydenham which her husband who was to be, talked of taking, she would be able to surround her father with every comfort, perhaps hire a phaeton, occasionally to drive him out; get him soup, wine, grapes, something in addition to the milk and eggs and their ordinary bare diet.

But the next morning he did not seem inclined to get up, and when Mr. Lacere came he went for a doctor.

The doctor asked a few questions, which Glen answered, though she did not exactly understand, and went away, saying he would send something round.

After that the girl never could exactly remember the sequence of events. Her whole time was taken up in nursing, and in learning how to cook for the sick. The hours passed, the days, the weeks, the months. It was the dead of winter. To herself she never seemed to have slept, or eaten, or rested during all that period. She was fighting death; but death wins in the long-run, do what we will.

Mr. Lacere lokoed on the struggle appalled. This was a catastrophe the near probability of which had never occurred to him.

' Glen, dear,' he entreated, ' marry me now. Give me the right to be near you, no matter what happens.'

But Glen laughed him to scorn. Nothing should happen. She would save her father. How could he ask her to leave that sick-room to go and be married to him ?

' My love, my darling, I only want to be able to call you my wife. I won't ask you to steal even one second from him to give to me.'

But she would not listen to his pleading. She was fighting—fighting every step of the way to the grave—and she could spare no time or thought for anything save that terrible campaign.

For which, as is the case in most campaigns, money was absolutely necessary, and her store was getting very low. She went down to Mr. Vassett and offered him the book written amongst the Middlesex moors for the modest sum of fifty pounds. She was quite in earnest, she explained—and indeed the publisher, looking at her, could not doubt that fact—she wanted fifty pounds for it.

As might have been expected, Mr. Vassett did not see his way to complying with her request; so then and there she took the manuscript on to a great house, where she managed to obtain an interview with the reader. He was very courteous, and, though he did not hold out much hope of acceptance under any circumstances—for he knew Miss Westley's writings of old—still he promised to look at the book; and having done all she could for that day, Glen went back to her post.

Miss Lacere was with her, and shared some of those awful vigils the girl must otherwise have passed alone. Most of them she did so pass ; God only knew—God and herself—the misery of those nights when she watched beside one who scarcely recognised her; when she moistened the lips that had forgotten to smile on her; when she raised the head that had grown a dead-weight; when she replenished the fire which was burning low, and watched for the grey light of morning and prayed for dawn, and wrestled with the mystery of existence as Jacob did with his Maker.

But through all she failed to understand what the end must be. She never believed she was merely tending the slow flicker of an expiring lamp; hour by hour she clung to the hope the feeble flame would grow stronger, and that her father would come back out of the depths of that terrible illness to life, strength, and his daughter. Even the doctors had not the heart to tell her there was no hope whatever; if they had, she would not have believed them. They warned her of danger, but they never spoke of death. She was the only person that entered the sick-room who failed to realize there was but one change possible. And so the days went by, and the weeks, and Glen afterwards wondered —as we all do mercifully, only afterwards— how she found strength to pass through such an ordeal.

There came at last one evening a change which made her fear he was worse, and in hot haste she despatched a messenger for a great physician who had been a friend of her father's in the days before he was Westley of Glenarva, or married or ruined, or thought he should die in London lodgings with a daughter beside him almost distraught by grief.

This doctor had come to see him more than once, and in this crisis Glen felt sure the wisdom of the faculty was centred in him, and that he alone could tell her what she ought to do, and how her father was to be restored to health. She wrote a note, and bade the servant take a cab and tell the man to drive fast.

While she waited the post brought a letter, and mechanically almost—for she was in the state of mind when it seems as though nothing in the world could prove of interest save one absorbing subject—she tore open the envelope and carelessly took out the enclosure.

It was from the reader of the great publishing firm where she had left her manuscript— and contained an acceptance of the novel!

For a minute she could not exactly understand this—the words seemed blurred, and the letters danced before her eyes—but at last she made out her book was thought highly of; and that if she would call and sign an agreement a cheque for twenty pounds would be handed to her in exchange.

Great heaven! she had waited all these years for this—and it came *then!*

She crossed the room, and kneeling down beside her father, said, ' Papa, can you understand me ? they have taken my book, and are to give me twenty pounds for it.'

She fancied—but it could only have been fancy—that his eyes turned towards her for a moment with a gleam of pleasure in them. 'Oh !' she cried passionately, ' if you would only get well now, papa—only get strong and well—how happy we might be !' And then her thoughts reverted to the great physician, and she marvelled how much more time would elapse before he came.

There was a dinner-party at his house, so the servant said when she returned, 'but the butler took the note to him, and he sent out word he would be round early to-morrow morning.'

'Go for another doctor,' that was all Glen said; '*any* doctor, only don't come back without one.'

Meanwhile at that dinner-table, of which the servant's eyes had caught through the open door one bewildering glance, the celebrated physician had remarked to a gentleman who sat near him :

'I don't know whether you remember Westley, who was with Lord Thanet's cousin at Rome. That note was from his daughter. Poor fellow ! the sands of his life are almost run out.'

'Westley !' repeated the other; 'why, Lord Thanet tried to find him everywhere more than a year ago. He got him an appointment, and I wrote myself saying how glad the Earl felt. The letter was returned by the post-office people, and we have never heard a word from him since.'

'Well, it is quite certain you will never hear from him now. He consulted me some months ago, and I then saw the case was hopeless. Still, I did not expect he would go off quite so soon. He is dying; there can't be a doubt of that.'

This was how it happened, that next morning, when the physician drove up to the house where Mr. Westley lodged, he found Lord Thanet turning away from the door.

'It is all over,' said the Earl.

'Ah! I thought the end could not be far off. I'll just go in and speak to the daughter.'

'I asked for her, but she cannot see anyone. A gentleman came down and told me so.'

CHAPTER XI.

MARRIED.

A BRIGHT summer's day in the August
following Mr. Westley's death;
high water in the river; the
Thames looking its very best—no sign of
mud-banks or bleak black shore—white sails
dotting the wide expanse of rippling blue, a
pleasant breeze blowing off the German Ocean,
and on the rising ground above Leigh, at the
foot of which that village nestles, Glenarva
Westley and Ned Beattie seated on the grass,
their eyes idly wandering over the landscape,
and their hearts almost too full for words,
busy with the past which had been theirs once
—but which could belong to them again no
more for ever.

Glen was visiting the curate and his wife, whose acquaintance she had made amongst the Middlesex moors. He was now rector of a scattered parish lying back in the lonely country, away from the river; and it was a pleasure in that desolate place to receive even so quiet a guest as the girl who, dressed in her deep mourning, sat often on Sundays in the great square pew belonging to the rector, looking with eyes that seemed drawn to it by some sort of fascination at the east window, which was the glory of the church, which people came from far and near to see, and which was, in its way, at once a triumph of art and a specimen of splendid colouring, such as modern mediocrity contemplated with despairing envy. The subject was the woman washing our Lord's feet with her tears, and often, as she gazed upon it, Glen found her own starting in sorrow for the sinner who, more than eighteen centuries before, stood in an agony behind her Saviour—weeping.

In the fine summer weather, Ned, coming from London to see his old companion, was invited to remain for a day or two; and thus it came to pass Glen had walked across country to show him the river and the ruins of Hadleigh Castle, and now they were resting on the heights above Leigh, and thinking of other days and far different scenes.

It was Ned who broke the silence. Stretch ing himself at full length on the grass, putting his hands under his head, and tilting his straw hat a little over his eyes, he said, evidently in resumption of some previous conversation :

'Glen, do you really mean to tell me none of your people ever did a single thing for you after your father's death ?'

Glen turned a thoughtful face in his direc-tion as she answered :

'Lady Emily wrote me word she had some black things, "almost as good as new," she could have packed up for me if I knew any-one who would bring them over; and Mrs. Westley——'

'Stop a minute,' entreated Ned, raising his head a little and bursting into a hearty fit of laughter. 'Kindly repeat that sentence; it sounds almost too funny to be true.'

'It is perfectly true,' answered Glen; 'and Mrs. Westley sent me a letter stating she supposed I had long before given up the disreputable idea of earning my living by writing mischievous and frivolous books, and that if I thought of qualifying myself to be a governess she was willing to let me try and teach her two little girls, and as I was a relative, would make me a present of ten pounds. I had committed a great sin, it seemed, in wanting to have my father buried at home. but she would " overlook my folly," she said, " knowing how badly I was brought up." '

' You must be inventing this, Glen, as you go on.'

' I should invent something pleasanter if I was inventing at all, you may be very sure of that. I'd say, for example, Lady Emily enclosed a cheque for a hundred pounds, and that my cousins asked me to pay a visit to Glenarva, and stay as long as I liked—as your mother invited me, Ned, to Ballyshane.'

' And why did you not come to us ?'

' For several reasons—one because I thought it would break my heart ; another that I could not spare the money ; and the third that I found I must stop near London. The publishers are worse than any *leprechaun*, Ned.

If you take your eyes off them for a minute they are lost.'

'Or, rather, the author is, I suppose,' answered Ned. 'And so it is a fact accomplished that you are an author, my dear.'

'Even so, Ned.'

'And is the game worth the candle?'

'It is generally admitted that one must live, and I have made enough to live on this year.'

'Have you really? Well, I suppose that is better than governessing, even at Glenarva?'

'A good deal, I should say.'

'They have cut the trees down in front of the house to open up a view of the Bay, and thinned the branches so as to let daylight in along the avenue. It is an improvement, I dare say, but I liked the look of the old place as it was best.'

'I never talk nor think about Glenarva, Ned, now, if I can help it.'

And silence reigned once more.

'I read that book of yours, Glen, 'Tyrrel's Son.' It was again young Beattie who broke the stillness. 'Aunt Stanuel brought it over with her. I did not think it so bad, at all.'

' Did you not ? That's consolatory,' observed the author.

' No ; I considered it good on the whole— good, that is, for a girl. Of course, women can't be expected ever to know anything of life.'

For a second Glen remained speechless with indignation ; then she retorted :

' If you mean the very disreputable sort of life you are best acquainted with, I am thankful to say I do not ; but of a better kind I know far more than Mr. Edward Beattie.'

Mr. Edward Beattie raised himself lazily on one elbow, and looked at her in amazement.

' Why, Glen,' he exclaimed, 'do you imagine I am leading a disreputable life ? It strikes me, young lady, your temper has got shorter even than it used to be at Ballyshane ; but don't let us quarrel, and for mercy's sake don't imply things you know are untrue.'

' Well, Ned, you *must* confess it is not true to say I know less of life than you.'

' I shall confess nothing of the sort. What *can* a woman know of life ? How is she to get to know it ? I'll be bound I have seen more of London since I came over last month than you during all the time you have lived in it.'

' Perhaps so,' answered Glen, with a smile of contempt.

' What are you writing now ?'

' A little story suited to the comprehension of children about five years of age,' with withering irony.

' Ah, then, it won't suit me,' said Ned resignedly, and he laid his head down again.

Glen contemplated her old companion stretched thus at his ease on the grass. He was not much changed, yet he had changed. It seemed to her he had grown strangely tall and manly since they were boy and girl together. There was a down on his upper lip, which she remembered smooth as her own. He had developed physically in a way which she thought little less than extraordinary, whilst his manner, never lacking in force and decision, had now a something of masculine strength and power added that struck Glen as almost unpleasant in its careless determination.

Nevertheless, young or old, tall or short, masterful or standing on an equality with herself, he was the dear Ned of the happy, vanished long ago, the Ned she had ridden with, walked with, climbed with, boated with, read with, quarrelled with, faced danger with, nursed, tended, loved.

As she looked, as fond memory laid its gentle hand on her heart, which had been so cruelly torn by time and circumstance, Glen's thoughts softened, and she felt sorry for having spoken even one sharp word to Ned, who she knew quite well never could mean to vex her. Already, as was usual with Glenarva Westley, the process of repentance had begun immediately. In the years then stretching before her, when Ned had forgotten all about her little temper, she knew she would suddenly remember that on the heights above Leigh she had been cross with her earliest friend.

Surreptitiously Ned, from under the sheltering brim of his straw hat, was out of the corner of one shrewd blue eye watching her.

He knew—none better—Glen's every mood and tense; he understood her, not with a comprehension born of any great power of mental analysis, but with a lore caused by a

power of perception in which few Irish men and
women are deficient he was perfectly aware that,
sooner even than usual, she was ready figura-
tively to kiss and be friends; that was all
right—but he could not fail to see something
else about Glenarva which puzzled and perplexed him. *She* had no down on her upper
lip ; *she* was not a bit taller or fatter or older-
looking than of yore ; her manner had not
changed in the least ; her little trumpery
success had not made or marred her, and
yet——

'Glen,' he said at last, ' is it at all likely
you will be in London before I leave ?'

With a start Glen returned to the questions of everyday life, and answered, 'Certain.'

' Where shall I be able to find you ?'

' At the Laceres'.'

' Oh ! you've spent a good deal of time with
them since—since last winter.'

' Yes, Ned.'

' Are they a pleasant family ?'

'They are exceedingly good-natured.'

' It seems to me you have formed a great
many acquaintances since you came to London.'

' I have met with a great deal of kindness,

if that is what you mean,' answered Glenarva gravely. Often in London she had not felt very grateful for the exceptional kindness which had been extended to her; but now, when she was well out of the toil and turmoil of the gigantic city—the noise and bustle of the busy streets—and found time to think, she could not help but be thankful for the genial words which had been spoken, and the kindly hands held out in greeting. Youth is all too apt to take such words and help for granted, but Glen, who was getting old—quite old—though still not out of her teens, could, when she found adequate leisure, afford to consider them.

For Glenarva came of a grateful stock. It was not in the nature of those from whom she drew life to forget the gift even of a cup of cold water, or a morsel of bread.

'Glen! did my mother tell you Aunt Louisa had left me a thousand pounds?' It was Ned who, from under cover of his straw-brimmed hat, put this question.

In reply Glen shook her head; though she gazed with quite a new and wondering interest at her old playfellow.

'Why don't you ask me what I am going to do with it?'

'What *are* you going to do with it?'

'I think of emigrating, or of taking a farm at home. Which course should you recommend?'

'If I were you, I should emigrate.'

Ned paused and considered this reply ere he remarked:

'I should want a wife to take out with me.'

'A wife!' screamed Glen. 'A boy like you with a wife!'

'Do you think I am too young to be married, then?' asked Ned. 'I am fourteen months older than you.'

'Of course you are.'

'And do you imagine you are too young to be married?'

'No. If you remember I told you once I met at Lady Emily's a Mrs. Betheling, who was a wife, a mother, and a widow before her seventeenth birthday.'

'She married again, I suppose, immediately.'

'No, she did not marry again at all.'

'Had enough, even in so short a time, of the holy state,' suggested Ned.

' I know nothing about that.'

' At all events you think a girl may marry before she is out of her teens ?'

' Of course I do ; don't you ?'

'The sooner a girl marries the better, I should say.'

' I feel very glad to hear that is your opinion, Ned, because I am going to be married.'

' You are going to be what ?' He was sitting bolt upright now, his hat lying on the grass beside him—the wind tossing his hair—looking straight at Glen.

' Married next month.'

' Oh ! indeed !'

' I should have been married nearly a year ago—only——'

' Is it indiscreet to ask the name of the happy man ?'

' No, Ned ; he is called Mordaunt Logan-Lacere.'

' Lacere ! By Jove ! I thought there must be something in it. And ink and paper were so scarce, I suppose, and postage so dear, you could not have told us this sooner.'

' I do not know why I have told you now.'

'It has slipped out just by accident! But for a mere chance we should have heard nothing about it till we read the announce- ment in the *Times* of Mordaunt Logan-Lacere being united in the bonds of. matrimony to Glenarva, only daughter, etc., etc. !'

'I don't see,' retorted 'Glenarva, only daughter, etc.,' 'what there is in being married to make a song about, as old Betty used to say.'

'Faith, in some cases a dirge might be more fitting,' returned Ned, as he gathered his long length up from the turf and walked away from Glen to a distant point, where he stood for a while, his hands deep in the pockets of his loose grey suit, apparently con- templating the view.

Stretching out her arm, Glen took up Ned's hat, which he had left unheeded on the grass, and began to smooth out the dark blue ribbon which encircled it, the time her thoughts went back to the many, many days she had seen just such another hat encircled by just such another ribbon shading a boy's honest sun- burnt face as he shouted out her name on shore, on sea, on cliff, on bog, at Ballyshane.

As she passed her fingers over and over the narrow silken band, tears rose unbidden to her eyes, and coursed one by one slowly down her cheeks. Had she been looking at the river she could not have seen it for that mist of inexplicable trouble. She had gone a long, long journey back into what seemed to her a far-distant past, and in spirit she was travelling the well-remembered paths once more, when a tall figure threw its shadow on the sward, and Ned again stood beside her.

'Glen,' he said, and all bitterness had died out of his voice, in which, however, there was a ring of pain, 'what is there in this marriage that you never told your best friends a word about it?'

'My best friend knew all about it,' she answered.

'You mean your father. Did he then approve the match?'

'Fully.'

'And how long have you known—a—Mr. Lacere?'

'Ever since the first winter we were in London.'

'So that all the time we were pitying " poor Glen," and thinking how lonely she must be, Glen had got plenty of friends, and was enjoying herself very much indeed?'

Glen sat silent. The false indictment was nothing, but had she opened her lips in defence, the memory of all she passed through during the period Ned thus lightly described as one of unalloyed enjoyment must have broken her down.

'I suppose he is disgustingly rich,' went on her tormentor, after he had for a moment waited in vain for a reply.

'No, he is not rich '

'That is, not rich for England, but still what we in Ireland should account a sort of millionnaire?'

'Have it your way, Ned,' answered Glen quietly.

'How old is he?'

'I don't exactly know.'

'Oh! come, Glen—that is too good. Give me an idea—is he older than I am?'

'Yes; he is older than you.'

'How much?'

'Ever so much.'

'Do you remember telling us all how you never would marry anybody ?'

' Yes ; but it's a free country, and besides, one knows what one is—but——'

'You certainly did not know what you might be,' finished Ned, with relentless decision. 'I told you once, if you recollect, you would marry your grandfather.'

Yes, Glen recollected, though she did not say so. Across the years there came to her a whiff of sweetbriar, and the scent of a lavender-bush growing within the Vicarage garden, where she and the boys stood talking about the grey-haired hero who had lunched that day with Mr. Beattie.

' We ought to be thinking about going home,' she said, after a pause.

'Not just yet,' he objected. 'When did you tell me the great event was to come off ?'

' Next month. I don't exactly yet know which day.'

' Is our friend of the parsonage to act as chaplain at the gallows ?'

' No.'

' Who is to tie the knot, then ?'

' I haven't an idea—anybody.'

'Well, you are a funny girl—I don't believe you care a bit for the man you are going to marry.'

'Don't you, Ned?' There was something unutterably sad and weary in her voice as she spoke.

'See, Glen'—he had thrown himself once more on the grass, and was now leaning towards his companion—'give me your hand, and say this after me, then I won't trouble you any more: "I'm so fond of the person I have chosen, I would take him if he had not a penny, and I feel I can trust the whole of my future life to his keeping."'

'God knows I can!' she added, when she had repeated this strange formula; and then, as Ned slowly released her hand, she covered her face for a minute ere, rising, she said: 'Now we had better go home.'

'Come down to the river,' he amended, 'and let us see if we can get a boat. It may be many a long day before I shall have a chance of rowing you again.'

Along the grass and down the steep hill they went, silently, side by side, together, and it was not till they were standing at a little shelving landing-place, waiting for a boat to be brought round, that Ned spoke again.

'Wouldn't it be better, Glen, for you to come back with me to Ballyshane, and let my father do all that is necessary under the circumstances?'

She shook her head, and answered, 'I would rather be married in London.'

A minute more and they were on the river —water all around them—the outward-bound ships making their way slowly against wind and tide, the Thames like a sheet of molten gold—the August sun westering over London, where the man Ned imagined to be 'disgustingly rich' was sitting in his quiet office, pondering 'ways and means.'

'Do you remember, Glen, the time I fell and broke my leg?' asked Ned, holding his sculls suspended for the moment as he asked the question.

'Of course I do,' she answered, watching the pearly drops falling like summer rain into the water.

'And that afternoon I bade you good-bye on board the Morecambe steamer?'

'Yes, Ned.'

'And when the years have come and gone, you will not forget to-day, and how everything looked from the heights yonder, and the way the sun shone on the water, and the shadows stealing round the church tower?'

'I shall not forget,' and she turned her head aside while he rowed steadily on.

'If I call I suppose I may be allowed to see you in London?' he said, as an hour and more later they walked in the evening light across the lonely wolds almost in utter silence.

'Of course! They will make any friend of mine welcome.'

'Where did you say Mr. Lacere has his office, Glen?'

'In Sise Lane.'

August was past, and September had come ere Ned, still wearing that unconventional straw hat and loose grey suit, on both of which Miss Humphries looked with distinct disfavour, paid his promised visit to the future Mrs. Lacere. When he called it was afternoon, and all the existing ladies of the Lacere family were in evidence. Glen had long ceased to count how many were dead as a vain and profitless calculation.

Looking round the quartet—to each one of whom he was duly and specially introduced—Ned irreverently summed them up in the same terms as a deceased Lord Abercorn is stated to have stigmatized two distinguished authoresses of his period, while it is only fair to say that the impression produced by Mr. Beattie was as little favourable as that made on him by Mr. Lacere's female relations.

He was asked to partake of tea, and, accepting the invitation, endeavoured to talk on such subjects as he supposed might prove agreeable to ladies, all of whom were old enough to be his mother, while one of them might, as he subsequently expressed the matter, 'have counted years, and won, with Miss Stanuel herself.'

It was after Miss Humphries had said solemnly, 'Will you allow me to give you another cup of tea, Mr. Beattie?' and Mr. Beattie, who was accustomed to take a great many cups of tea, had answered, 'Yes, thank you,' that he proceeded to scandalize all the ideas of the Lacere connection by remarking across the table :

'Well, Glen, I took Sise Lane on my way here, and saw your man.'

Glen felt the startled chill which for a moment froze the blood of her relatives who were to be, at Ned's free-and-easy designation of Mordaunt Logan-Lacere, but she answered :

'Did you ? I hope you were pleased with each other.'

'I was pleased with him,' said Ned, taking no notice of the stony looks of disapproval with which his utterances were received ; 'we had a long talk. I dare say I stopped there an hour. I told him I hoped he would not let you get your head.'

Glen smiled. 'And what is his notion on the subject ?'

'The usual thing, of course,' replied Ned. 'Thinks you would be sure to go right—without bit, bridle, or curb. "Very well," I said, "do as you like ; but remember I knew her before ever you did, and the very best thing for both of you will be to keep her well in hand." '

'It seems to me, Mr. Beattie, your advice, however admirable, has the great drawback of being somewhat obscure,' remarked Miss Lacere, with great dignity.

'Oh ! he knew well enough what I meant,

and so does Glen,' returned Ned, as if it were of no consequence whatever whether Miss Lacere were similarly fortunate or not.

'I suppose the old girls will be kind to you,' he said, as he and Glen strolled together towards the Regent's Park. He had suggested she should put on her bonnet and walk part of the way back with him.   'They seem inclined to make a great fuss over their new sister-in-law.'

'Yes, they have been very kind to me,' answered Glen.

'That other Lacere is a very velvety-spoken sort of individual.   He thinks, I fancy, he has got a monopoly of all the virtues, as well as all the talents.'

'I can't tell, I am sure.'

Meantime there was quite a flutter going on in the Lacere dovecote.

'I don't approve of that young man's manners at all, Glen,' observed Miss Lacere when Glen, looking a little pale, returned home and took a seat as far distant from the chandelier as possible.

'Don't you?' asked the girl.

'No, indeed! Fancy him talking of our

precious blessing as " your man," and hoping he
would not let you " get your head !" '

' Poor Ned !'

Already Glen had a feeling no friend of hers
would meet with much favour in that household. ' But it does not much matter,' she
thought. She felt strangely tired and peace-
ably minded.

' I wish I had married a year ago,' she
decided ; and undoubtedly it would have been
much better, as no one knew more certainly
than Mr. Logan-Lacere himself.

Though late, however, the wedding-day
dawned at last, a dull morning, obscured by a
damp mist which resolved itself before the ap-
pointed hour into a wretched drizzling rain.

Unless they had walked into church alone
together, no pair could have been married more
quietly.

One of the Misses Lacere for bridesmaid,
Mr. Lacere for best-man, a gentleman who was
a stranger to Ned for father—that was all the
wedding-party.

In a half-hearted sort of way Glen had asked
young Mr. Beattie to be present, but he refused
on the ground that he was leaving London.

Nevertheless, though she did not see him, her old friend was there, and as he walked from the church to Euston Square Station he shook his head once or twice mournfully.

'It was as sad a ceremony as I ever need desire to witness,' he thought; 'yet if they are unhappy I am sure the fault will not be his.'

END OF VOL. II.

BILLING AND SONS, PRINTERS, GUILDFORD AND LONDON.

G., C. & Co.